D0117849

UNCERTAIN JOY

UNCERTAIN JOY

Hilary Wilde

CHIVERS
THORNDIKE

This Large Print edition is published by BBC Audiobooks Ltd, Bath, England and by Thorndike Press®, Waterville, Maine, USA.

Published in 2004 in the U.K. by arrangement with Juliet Burton Literary Agency.

Published in 2004 in the U.S. by arrangement with Juliet Burton Literary Agency.

U.K. Hardcover ISBN 0–7540–9982–2 (Chivers Large Print)
U.K. Softcover   ISBN 0–7540–9983–0 (Camden Large Print)
U.S. Softcover   ISBN 0–7862–6305–9 (Nightingale)

The text of this Large Print edition is unabridged.
Other aspects of the book may vary from the original edition.

Set in 16 pt. New Times Roman.

Printed in Great Britain on acid-free paper.

British Library Cataloguing in Publication Data available

Library of Congress Control Number: 2003116431

CHAPTER ONE

Penny Trecannon hurried home through the pelting rain from South Kensington station to the small flat she shared with her father and stepmother. It was a cold evening and she was tired, and miserable, because her boss had asked why she was suddenly making spelling mistakes and forgetting things.

'It's not like you,' he had said. 'What's wrong?'

So she had told him. 'Since Dad married again, I've felt . . . well, I've felt I'm the odd one out. When Mum died Dad turned to me. I've always adored him and maybe I should be ashamed, and I am, but I'm just plain jealous. Fiona, you see, is only about three years older than me and . . .'

'You poor kid,' the boss had said. 'You should get another job—in another town, maybe another country.

'But I don't want to leave Dad . . .' she had begun, and then saw the look on his face. 'I know,' she had added. 'I'm being just plain selfish.'

It was true, too. Dad was so much happier since he married Fiona—and Fiona was super; apart from being most attractive, she was kindness itself, but did they really want a third person with them?

1

Penny let herself into the flat. Fiona came running down the hall, her long dark hair swinging, her face eager.

'Oh, Penny, I'm glad you're back—I need your help. You know the Favershams? At least, you've heard of them. Your father and I play bridge with them. Well, they've got a very important friend coming—a Spanish millionaire—and are taking him out to dinner. Their usual baby-sitter is sick and they can't get another, so they asked me to go, but your father has got tickets for us to go to the theatre and it's a super comedy. Have you a date for tonight?'

'No.' Penny made herself smile, hoping Fiona would not see how it hurt when Dad took Fiona out alone, leaving his own daughter behind. Not that he always left her behind, but he took it for granted she had friends she wanted to be with. She had a few, but she would have far preferred to be with him. 'Of course I'll baby-sit, but I don't know the child.'

'I'll give you the address. It's up near the Albert Hall. Bless you, Penny. They're such good friends I didn't like to let them down, but I didn't want to let your father down either. Have a quick bath and I'll cook you some supper and you have a taxi each way. They'll pay for them.' She went off to the kitchen, singing happily.

Penny hurried to her bedroom. She looked around the room thoughtfully. She and her

2

father had moved to this small flat after her mother died. It had been large enough for two of them, but three . . . That was a different story.

Half an hour later she got out of the taxi and went into the tall, impressive-looking marble-pillared building. The Favershams were on the fifth floor. As she rang the bell the door opened and a tall man let her in. He smiled. 'You're Jock Trecannon's daughter Penny?' he asked, shaking her hand warmly. 'He's always talking of you. Thinks the world of you, he does. I'm Reginald Faversham. We've got an important guest—an old friend but also a client.' He chuckled. 'Thanks for helping us out.'

Mrs. Faversham appeared, a small blonde woman with a grateful smile.

'We were feeling desperate. You can't just leave your child with anyone.'

She led the way into the luxurious sitting-room, switched on the television and poured out a glass of sherry.

'Little Estrella is in here,' she said, leading the way to the bedroom. A small four-year-old child lay asleep, her long black hair spread out over the white pillow case, her little face serene.

'The only thing is . . .' Penny hesitated, but went on. 'Won't she be frightened if she wakes up and finds a stranger here?'

'No one could be frightened of you, my

3

dear,' Mrs. Faversham said with a smile. 'She very rarely wakes up.'

Left alone, Penny curled up on the sofa, tossing off her shoes, watching the television yet seeing none of it, for her mind was too busy with her problem.

Was she being a nuisance to her father? Would they be happier if she left them? Only she'd have to do it so that they didn't think she had done it because of them—that would upset both Dad and Fiona. Penny closed her eyes, trying to imagine how they must feel. She had never been really in love; there had been a few boys she had liked very much, but after her mother's death she had rarely accepted invitations as she had hated leaving her father alone, and the boys got tired of rejections and dropped her. But none of them had she really *loved*—that was something quite different. Fiona really loved her husband, Penny knew that—and Dad loved Fiona. And who could blame him when his young wife waited on him and fussed over him and made him feel young again despite his forty-four years?

Penny heard a sound and hurried to the bedroom. Little Estrella was crying, so Penny knelt by her side and took her in her arms.

'Did you have a nasty dream, darling?'

Estrella nodded and went on crying. Penny rocked her gently.

'I have dreams like that,' she said. 'But they're only dreams.'

'I thought 'twas true . . .'

It was half an hour before Estrella went to sleep, but she looked serene again with her little elfin face still and her hair spread out.

Penny fell asleep on the couch and woke with a start as she heard the door open and voices. She sat up, stifling a yawn, brushing back her long red hair and rubbing her green eyes.

Joan Faversham came in. 'I'm afraid we're very late, dear. How did things go?'

Penny was on her feet. 'She's fine. She woke up once with a nightmare. I said I had them, too. Then I told her stories and she went to sleep.'

'No trouble?'

Penny laughed. 'No trouble at all. She's sweet.' Reginald Faversham came in, too, followed by a man at whom Penny stared in amazement. He must be the Spanish millionaire—the Favershams' old friend—and he was a tall, lean man in his mid-thirties! She had expected an old man. He was the sort of man she had never seen before. His hair was dark and thick. His skin was olive, so were his eyes dark. Strange eyes that were looking at her in an odd way—as if he was questioning her, trying to read her thoughts.

Reginald Faversham introduced him to her. 'This is Señor Juan del Riego,' he said, 'an old friend of ours. Juan, this is the daughter of a friend, Penny Trecannon. She's very kindly

5

been baby-sitting for us. I'll run you home, my dear.'

Juan del Riego spoke quickly. 'If I may suggest it, it would be more simple for me to drive the young lady home. It is no hardship,' he added, his eyes amused.

'That's fine,' said Joan Faversham. 'It's near South Kensington station—Penny will tell you. Thank you so much, my dear.'

'I enjoyed it,' Penny said with a smile.

She went with the Spaniard down in the lift. They did not speak as he took her to his car, a huge white one with a yawning chauffeur jumping out and coming to open the car door.

'What is your address?' Juan del Riego asked. Penny told the chauffeur and he nodded, he knew the road well.

'It was good of you to help my friends. They are devoted to their little girl,' Juan del Riego said. He was elegantly dressed but not over-dressed, she thought. Very polite, if only he would not keep staring at her in that odd fashion, as if he wanted to discover something in her or find an answer to a question he had in mind. It made her feel uncomfortable.

He escorted her politely to her door, waited until she had unlocked it and held out his hand. She thought he was going to shake hers, but instead he bent and kissed it.

'It has been a pleasure to meet you, Miss Trecannon. We shall meet again,' he said politely, then turned and left her.

6

She went into the flat, closing the door gently, for her father was a light sleeper. In her own room, she hurriedly undressed and got into bed. What a nice couple the Favershams were, no wonder Dad liked them. And Estrella was a little darling. And the Spanish millionaire . . . like someone from another world with that old-fashioned courtesy. What had he meant when he said: 'We'll meet again'? When would they? How—where?

*   *   *

It was three o'clock before Penny fell asleep, so next day she overslept. Fiona woke her at ten o'clock with breakfast on a tray.

'How did you get on?' she asked.

'Fine.' Penny rubbed her sleepy eyes. 'Estrella is sweet.'

'And the millionaire?'

'An unusual sort of man. Most unusual. So polite—so . . .'

'Tell me later, love. I'm doing your father an omelette. He's got a bit of a cold and not much appetite, but I know he loves omelettes,' Fiona said, and disappeared.

Penny ate her breakfast, got up, showered and dressed. She didn't hurry, since there was no need. On Saturdays she always helped with the housework and had no reason to go out, and when Fiona came to the door and said in a strangely excited voice: 'There's a . . . there's someone to see you, Penny,' Penny didn't even bother to look in the mirror. It could only be Jill or Rosemary who lived round the corner coming to see her.

But as she followed Fiona to the sitting-room, she caught her breath, her hand flying to her untidy red hair and her shiny nose—for there stood Señor Juan del Riego.

She felt confused, for she knew she must look like something the cat found in the dustbin, as her mother would have said.

'I didn't . . . didn't know . . .' she stammered, looking down at the jeans and white shirt she was wearing. 'I overslept and . . .'

'That is obvious, Miss Trecannon. This is a business call and not a social one, so your appearance is not important, although in some ways it may be—but I will deal with that later. Is this how you always appear except when at a party? Last night you looked quite different.'

Her cheeks burning, she leapt to her own defence. 'Of course not. This is only when I'm at home and doing housework. Besides, last night it wasn't a party—I was baby-sitting.'

'Was that your real reason for being there? I mean, I wondered if you had arranged it in order to meet the famous Señor Juan del Riego?' He sounded amused.

Again Penny flushed. 'I'd never heard of you,' she began, then wondered if she was being rude. 'I'm sorry, but . . . but ought I to

8

have heard of you?'

How he laughed. He looked completely different. 'That is good, Miss Trecannon. Maybe you do not read the financial news or listen to the television interviews with international financiers. I am a very wealthy man, so usually I am well known and naturally always suspicious when I meet a charming girl like you.' He chuckled. 'I can see I was wrong, and I apologise. Perhaps you will understand that for a man of my kind, life is not always easy. Could I sit down?' he asked, his deep vibrant voice changing again.

'Of course. I'm so sorry . . .' said Penny, thinking that he was clever in making her feel uncomfortable and stupid. 'I'm sorry.'

Fiona spoke then from the doorway: 'Would you like some coffee?'

Penny turned and saw that Fiona was looking most strange, her face showing her surprise and dismay as if she couldn't understand what was going on.

Señor Riego gave a little bow. 'It would be most pleasant,' he said, and smiled.

It was the most amazing smile Penny had ever seen. Quite different from his look of amusement or his boisterous laughter, this was a smile that lightened his face, which had a squarish chin and a somewhat large nose.

As Fiona left the room, Juan del Riego gave a little bow to Penny, indicating a chair as he sat down. Penny also sat down hastily but on

9

the edge of an upright chair.

'You are fond of children?' he asked.

The question was unexpected, though he had been staring at her in such an odd manner that she had wondered what could be in his mind.

'Why . . . why, of course.'

'I can see no "of course" about it. Unfortunately I know quite a number of people who have no time for children. There is an old saying: *"Children are certain sorrow but only uncertain joy".*'

'Certain sorrow but uncertain joy . . .' Penny quoted, looking puzzled. 'I'm afraid I don't understand.'

'Neither do I,' he said with a short laugh. 'I believe it is a Swedish proverb.'

Fiona had brought in the tray and she spoke quickly.

'I think it's horrid. Making out that you may get some happiness but you're bound to get sorrow. I don't agree at all. I want children of my own.'

'That is good to hear. And you, Miss Trecannon?'

'I . . . I haven't thought about it,' Penny admitted.

'You have not thought of marriage and motherhood? Surely that is unusual?' He sounded as if he was condemning her, blaming her for not being a woman.

Fiona laughed. 'She's only nineteen, Señor

Riego, and has had no desire yet to marry.'

'Nineteen?' Juan del Riego repeated slowly, his eyes looking up and down Penny's slight body. She felt terrible, wanting to run to her room and put on something clean. What a sight she must look! 'I have a problem and I would like to tell you what it is,' he went on.

Fiona answered as she poured out the coffee. 'But of course. We shall be delighted to listen. Sometimes talking about it helps you find the solution,' she said almost gaily. She was looking prettier than ever, for she was a real extrovert, liking to meet people and talk to them. 'If only I was like that,' Penny was thinking.

Señor Juan del Riego smiled. 'You are so right. I must start a long way back. My Aunt Lucille met Fernando Dominguez when he was on a visit to England. His good looks and charm hid his narrow mind and his arrogant callousness. They married and had a son, Pedro. My mother went to stay with them on the island of Vallora . . .' He spoke proudly as if it was the only island of any importance in the world and that there was no need for him to name it. 'She was enchanted by my father.' There was a bitterness in his voice. 'Like all the family, he had great charm, unfortunately. What a mistake those two English girls made! You must understand that a Spaniard has firm ideas as to how his wife and children must behave, and this is not always in accordance

11

with the ideas of an English lady.' His hands moved expressively as he spoke and he smiled—that strange smile that changed his face and fascinated Penny.

'It is not always good to marry someone who has not your background, your training or your ideals. I am sad to say that both my mother and her sister were most unhappy and so were their children. It is these that should be considered before marriage is undertaken.' He frowned. 'I am very much against mixed marriages as it is not fair to the children.' Now he spoke curtly and he looked at Penny, a strange look that sent a cold shiver down her back. Was he trying to tell her something? Was he threatening her? Why—why? What had she done?

'Pedro, of whom I am speaking,' Señor del Riego went on, 'was a delicate child. He was a few years older than I, but we were always close friends. It is tragic when a father and mother do not live in harmony, but they did not. My uncle would not allow a word of English to be spoken, though my aunt did her best to teach Pedro a little, as much as she dared, for her husband had a bad temper. My uncle died and my aunt sent Pedro to a school in England. Life was difficult for that delicate child who found it hard to learn another language. I tell you all this so that you will understand later. He was unhappy at that school and has always said he will not allow it to happen to his children.

'I was more fortunate, for my mother was a stronger character than her sister. She taught me English from a child. This is what Pedro has said in his will . . .'

'He is dead?' Fiona sounded shocked.

'Unfortunately, yes. A tragic death after many years of illness. My parents had gone to South America to live. At one stage, Pedro was too ill to govern Vallora. He asked his cousin Alfonso Rodriguez Melado to take over, but Alfonso is the kind who expects to be given everything for doing nothing. He was leading a gay life and had no desire to work. So Pedro wrote to me and I went. I was on Vallora for five years until Pedro's health improved. This is why in his will . . .'

'Is it his will that's your problem?' Fiona asked, her face eager as she leaned forward.

His hands moved expressively. 'You are so right. It is his will. But I must shorten this long story.' He glanced at his wrist watch and nodded. 'I have much to do and little time in which to do it. I have changed my plans. I am now flying back to the island this afternoon.'

'Yes, the will . . .' Fiona repeated as if trying to hurry him as she poured out second cups of coffee. Fiona loved to listen to other people's problems, Penny thought affectionately. She herself was more fascinated by the man himself, the way he moved his hands, the changes in his face and in that deep vibrant

13

voice that had an arrogant tone one moment and a surprisingly gentle one the next.

'When my cousin died, he left a generous allowance for life for his wife—the rest was to go to his three children when they reached a certain age and I . . .' Señor del Riego paused dramatically, yet Penny knew he did not do it intentionally. He was not showing off, but this drama was part of his strange Spanish/English background.

'Pedro asked me to be guardian of his children and to look after the island which they would inherit. He also wished me to guard them from their uncle, Alfonso Melado, who believes that control of the island should be his and is determined to get it back again, no matter at what cost. Also to protect them from their mother, who has no time for children at all.'

For a moment Señor del Riego's expressive face looked tired. 'It is sad, so very sad, but on Vallora is much hatred and many feuds and little affection. It is a beautiful island, unique in appearance and with great potentiality, but they live in the past and have no desire to realise that today is very different. In the will, Pedro specifically asked me to insist that the children learn English at once. He had tried to insist, but in the last years he was too weak to succeed. He knew he could leave it to me. He said they must learn to speak English as small children. It is the only way. That is why I have

14

come to England, yet I have found no one suitable as a governess.' He turned to Penny, who was sitting silently. 'I am ashamed to say it, but while I loved my mother, I had no affection for my father. It is said this is purely biological—is it the same for you? Of course it will be in reverse. It must be your father you adore?'

'I . . . I . . .' Penny was startled by the sudden question. 'Yes, I do adore my father, but . . . but . . .'

'Her mother died only two years ago,' Fiona said quickly.

'I am so sorry.' Señor del Riego looked at Penny. 'Had I known I would not have asked you. I trust that you will forgive me?'

'Of course,' said Penny. 'In any case, I didn't hate my mother. She was very kind . . .'

'A real darling,' Fiona chimed in. 'I was jilted, brokenhearted.' She laughed. 'And your mother helped me so much, Penny.'

'I can imagine,' said Penny. So that was how her father had met Fiona. She had often wondered.

Fiona nodded. 'You were away at the time, staying with your friends at Yarmouth.' She turned to the man. 'I'm sorry we interrupted you. You were telling us . . .'

'Yes, of course. That I have been looking for a suitable governess—a quiet girl, not too young nor too old. Not flamboyant, or aggressive. Life on the island will not be easy.

Pedro's widow is against it, of course. But . . .'
His voice changed, became cold and almost
brutal as he went on: 'She will have to accept
it—I shall see to that. You are the one I have
chosen, Miss Trecannon.'

'Me? Chosen? I don't understand . . .' Penny
was startled and sat forward, nearly sliding off
the chair.

He looked at her. 'I have decided that
you are the most suitable. You cannot speak
Spanish?'

'Of course not! I've no idea . . .'

'Splendid. The children must find that they
have to speak English, and if you cannot speak
their language, they will have no choice.' In an
odd way, he clipped the words so that she
was reminded of a sergeant-major shouting
instructions on the parade-ground.

'But . . . you want *me*?' Penny almost gasped.
'I'm not a governess. I've had no experience.'

'Good.' He stood up. 'I do not want you to
be a governess but a friend. You are not
expected to teach them anything except
English. This is essential, as I have arranged
for those old enough to go to English boarding
schools as soon as possible.' As if he
remembered something, he sat down and
frowned. 'One thing I have forgotten. You
have a lover? Yes? I mean, you are not
engaged? In love?' He said the words almost
scornfully.

'No . . . no, but . . .'

16

'You seem perfect to me—a quiet girl, fond of children, yet also aware that discipline is sometimes necessary. I have decided . . .'

'But you don't know me, or . . .'

He smiled condescendingly. 'You forget, Miss Trecannon, that I am accustomed to dealing with people and I credit myself with the ability to judge character. I think you would be ideal.'

'But . . .'

Fiona leaned forward, her eyes sparkling. 'It sounds wonderful, *señor*. Penny is awfully good with children. You know you are, Penny. Remember the time we visited the Robinsons and how the children adored you?'

'Yes, but . . .'

Penny felt confused as she tried to sort out her thoughts. A job on some unknown island where there were feuds and hatred and a mother determined to fight every inch of the way—and three children being forced to learn to speak English—did she want such a job? Yet on the other hand, the happiness on Fiona's face told Penny so much, made her know that her fear was right and that she was being in their way, that their marriage could not be a perfect one so long as she stayed with them. Wasn't it natural for Fiona to want her husband all to herself—without a daughter always there? Whatever happened, though, no one must know the reason for Penny leaving home. All the same, such a job sounded terrifying.

Señor del Riego stood up. 'That is arranged. You will not become engaged for six months? Married for a year? I do not want the children to be confused by a different face. How soon can you come?'

'But I . . .' Penny began, but he was not listening.

'Ten days. That will give you time to hand in your notice and decide what to wear. In winter even the Mediterranean can be cold, so do not bring only thin garments. I would also repeat that jeans, trews, short skirts and bikinis are not accepted on Vallora. As I said, it is many years out of date and I want no danger of you causing scandalous gossip. I am prepared to pay you well . . .'

He mentioned a sum that made both Fiona and Penny gasp and then he went on: 'You will have the use of a carriage, as we have no cars on the island. You have a passport? Good. Then I will arrange for your flight to be booked and the tickets sent to you. You will be met at the small airport on Vallora.' He gave a strange smile. 'That is about the only modern thing on the island—and what a fight Pedro had to have it! Fortunately his ill-health which meant he had to go frequently to the mainland was a good reason.'

He turned to Fiona and bowed. 'It has been a delight to meet you. Perhaps you and your husband would care to come and visit your stepdaughter some time? You will always be welcome. By the way,' he turned back to Penny, 'a good deal of entertainment takes place on the island when we are talking to one another—' He gave a strange smile, then. 'It is advisable that you bring suitable clothes. A woman should look like a woman—discreet, feminine, attractive but modest . . .'

'But that's absurd . . .' Penny began indignantly.

'I agree, but when in Rome we must do as the Romans do. I do not want the relatives to be able to prove that you are unsuitable to take care of the children. They will be eager to find a reason for dismissing you, and this I will not allow.' He glanced at his wrist watch. 'I must go. I will see you in ten days.'

Fiona and Penny stood up. Señor del Riego took their hands, lightly kissing them and giving each one that amazing smile of his.

Once the door was closed, Penny kicked off her sandals and literally collapsed on the couch.

'Am I out of my mind?' she asked Fiona. 'Why did I give in? I don't want that sort of job. It was like a whirlwind—he just swept through giving me no chance to refuse. The families sound too ghastly for words . . . I can't wear jeans. I ask you! What right have they to lay down the law . . .' Her voice began to rise with the anger she had not been able to show while Señor del Riego was there.

19

Fiona curled up in a chair, laughing. 'Don't be daft, Penny. Imagine a beautiful island in the Mediterranean—think of palm trees, gorgeous sunshine. It'll be super. No real work, just talking to the children, and you know you love children.' She laughed. 'I think he's terribly attractive, don't you? We didn't ask him if he was married, but he did give you a sort of warning.'

'A warning?'

'Sure. Didn't you get it? He kept on about the foolishness of English girls marrying Spaniards, especially the kind on his island. In other words, don't fall in love with him.'

Penny laughed. 'Most unlikely. I admit I can't stop looking at him. He's got such an unusual face, it keeps changing all the time. All the same, I can't imagine falling in love with him . . . if anything he rather frightens me.'

'Frightens you? Are you out of your mind? He's an absolute darling. Look at his concern for his cousin's children. How many men would care? No, I think he's a honey and I think this is a wonderful chance for you, Penny dear. Your father is rather worried because you lead such a quiet life. He'd like you to meet other people of your age. There must be quite a lot on this island.' She jumped up. 'Look at the time, we'd better get to work.'

'Yes, we had,' said Penny, slowly rising. She shook her head so that her long red hair swung. 'I wonder he gave me the job when I look so awful.'

Fiona laughed, the gaiety alive in it. 'Nonsense! Nothing could make you look awful, Penny. You have a strange beauty that isn't, if you know what I mean.'

'He does rather lay down the law.'

'Of course he does. That's how he's become a millionaire.'

CHAPTER TWO

Penny found herself flying high across Spain exactly ten days later, finally landing at Barcelona airport. Everything had gone smoothly, apart from the misery inside her. Oddly enough her father hadn't approved at first about the job.

'As far away as that,' he had said. 'Who is the man? Some foreigner? No, definitely no.'

How Fiona had laughed! 'Jock, Penny is no baby. If she wants to go, let her. Ring up the Favershams and they'll tell you about him.'

He had done so and come back from the phone, smiling.

'You're right as usual, Fiona, and I was wrong. It seems Señor del Riego is a highly respected man and the Favershams have known him for years. This island is not his—he merely owns a lease that has gone on for centuries, and it's all very beautiful. The Favershams have been there and seem to think you'll enjoy yourself. If you *really* want to go?' he had asked, a faint note of sorrow in his voice, and for a moment Penny had to battle with the desire to throw herself in his arms and hug him tight while she cried—as she had often done in the past—saying she didn't want to leave him. But she knew that would be wrong of her. Her father and Fiona loved one another—if their marriage was to be a success it must be a happy companionship, and how could it be with a grown-up daughter always around?

'I think it might be fun, Dad,' she said. 'He's invited you and Fiona to visit me.'

Her father's face brightened. 'We'll do that, my darling, we surely will,' he had said, and hugged her close.

So Fiona and she had gone shopping, Fiona joking about it while Penny's misery had grown as the days passed. And then had come that last farewell when her father had driven her to Heathrow and said goodbye. Somehow she had managed not to cry, but she felt terribly alone as she found her place on the plane. It was crowded, mostly with people going in search of the sun for their yearly holiday, but Penny had sat, arms folded, eyes closed, as she thought of her father going home to Fiona . . .

Home! Anywhere with Dad had been home to Penny. This was really the first time she had ever been away from home for any length of time. Six months, perhaps a year, was a long time.

At the airport she felt bewildered as she looked at the swirling crowd of laughing, chattering tourists and saw them gathering in queues. She looked at the second ticket that would take her to Vallora, and then vaguely around. As usual she felt lost. Her father had always said she wasn't observant and her

23

mother had joked and said Penny lived in a dream world, but now here she was!

'Excuse me, but have you lost something?' a man asked.

Startled, she turned round. A short lean man was looking at her worriedly.

'No,' she told him. 'Except I don't know where to go.'

He smiled. He had a pleasant long face and his blue eyes were friendly. 'Where are you going?'

She told him and he laughed. 'An easy solution. I'm going there, too.'

She was so relieved. 'I know it's stupid of me, but I always get lost in places like this. It's so crowded and . . .'

'This way,' he said. 'Have you got your luggage? And your ticket? Where have you come from? London? I was there a couple of months ago and . . .'

He was still talking as they settled down in their seats in the small plane. Penny was glad to have his company, for it had removed some of the miserable loneliness she had felt before.

'If I may ask, what are you doing on Vallora?' her new friend asked.

'I've come to teach the children English.'

'Phew!' he whistled softly. 'That won't be easy.'

'So Señor Juan del Riego said, but he also said it was his cousin's wish for his children. They seem to mean a lot to him.'

Michael Trent—for that was his name, he had told her—smiled.

'Do they, now? I'm an accountant, engaged by him because he has only recently taken over the island, and he has an idea that something fishy has been going on. My job is to audit everything—not easy when so many members of the family are involved, and they're hostility itself.'

'He said there were many feuds and much hatred.'

'The understatement of the year! They all hate one another and remember things that happened centuries ago. For instance, they hate us—us English, I mean—because in the sixteenth and seventeenth centuries they were corsairs or pirates and penetrated into English and Irish waters. These people have centuries-long family trees and several of their ancestors were killed by the English, so they'll always hate us. I ask you!' He laughed. 'Fancy going back so far. It's just plain stupid.'

'He said they were years out of date.'

'And that's true. They're a funny lot.'

The plane had taken off and soon they were high above the blue Mediterranean. The sun was shining, the clouds white and puffy below them and suddenly the plane, with its few passengers, most of them elderly, began to circle as it went down. There below in the water was a strange-looking island. There was a large cluster of mountains in the middle with

25

a long narrow promontory at either end.

'It's completely out of date as regards economics,' Michael Trent said. 'Where those long strips are, they grow grapes and apples. That lump in the middle is chiefly for sheep, most of the houses are there, too, but parts of the mountains are blackened still from the lava of a volcano some hundred years ago. There are minerals there, but the family won't get out of their houses. They say they've lived there for centuries. They can't realise they don't *own* the land. Not that Riego does. It's merely leased as it has been for several centuries. One of these days, the Spanish Government will realise that a little fortune is waiting here and then the families will have to get out, like it or not. They're a funny crowd. Some are charming and friendly, others don't even look at you. You won't have an easy time.'

Penny gave a little laugh. 'I'm aware of that.'

They were circling as they went lower and lower and she could see that the island was bigger than it had first looked. As the plane slowed up and slid along the air-strip she could see the enormous mountains towering above the flat land.

As she got out of the plane with Michael Trent by her side, she saw Juan del Riego. He was frowning, but as they joined him, he curtly nodded to Michael Trent and said with a stiff politeness to Penny:

'I trust you had a pleasant journey, Miss

26

Trecannon. No problems?'

She sensed his disapproval. Was it because she had travelled with Michael Trent? Surely not. Yet it wasn't his fault, she thought, so she said quickly:

'Everything was fine, but I got a bit lost about flying out to your island. I couldn't find where the plane was, but Mr. Trent helped me.'

'How very kind of him,' Señor del Riego said slowly, his voice hard. 'How did you get on, Trent?'

'I managed to see several of them, but two were away...' Michael Trent began, but Señor del Riego lifted his hand.

'No details now. I'll see you in two hours' time in your office.'

'Right, sir.' Michael Trent smiled at Penny. 'See you,' he said cheerfully, and before he left them, smiled at Penny: 'Good luck.'

Penny was looking round. How flat this part of the island was—or was it because of the height of the range of mountains that towered above them?

'How long have you known Michael Trent?' the Señor asked, his voice cold. Startled, she looked at him.

'About an hour.'

'You didn't know him before you came?'

'Of course not.' She was suddenly annoyed. 'Are you calling me a liar?'

'I merely wondered if that was why you took

27

the job. To be near him.'

'I told you—I didn't know him.'

'Then why did you take the job? I could see you hesitated, in fact it was obvious that you did not want it, so why did you?'

'That's my business,' she began angrily, then shrugged. 'All right, if you want to know, I . . . I felt my father and Fiona ought to be alone. They haven't been married long and . . . and . . .'

'You felt in the way? You probably were. I see. Thank you.'

'You believe me?' She looked up at him as he stood by her side. His hands were linked behind his back, his neat suit spotlessly clean, his shoes shining in the sunlight, his eyes as full of questions as she had noticed before.

'Why not? I must explain a few things, Miss Trecannon. Here on this island, and indeed in most parts of Spain, girls before they are married are not given the freedom of girls in England. Therefore when an English girl comes out and is allowed to roam alone where she likes or mix with some doubtful characters, it is only natural that she is given a bad name. I do not wish this to happen to you. You will be in charge of the children and your character must be absolutely blameless in every way.'

'Are you suggesting Michael Trent is a doubtful character?' Penny asked, angry again.

Juan del Riego's face changed as he smiled. 'No, I am not. But please remember that here

28

you will have many enemies, looking carefully at you, waiting—and hoping—that you will do something foolish so that they can get rid of you.'

Penny drew herself up, lifting her small pointed chin. 'You would let them?' she asked accusingly.

'Of course not, but it could be unpleasant for you. I would prefer you to keep out of such trouble.'

He stopped talking and led the way to a big black carriage with two horses impatiently fidgeting. A man in a white jacket and trousers slid down and opened the carriage door, while Juan del Riego helped her in. She looked round her.

He smiled. 'Just as if you'd gone back to Victorian days?' he asked.

'It seems right here, somehow.'

Penny could see how the vines grew on either side of the road, standing tall and methodically straight like soldiers on parade. Everything looked so neat. There were large orchards of apple trees, as well. As far as she could see over this long narrow promontory, there was only one road, wide and earthy, along which the horses trotted happily.

'We are approaching one of the two towns on the island. You will notice that there is a considerable amount of Moorish architecture. Many years ago there was Moorish occupation and they have left many evidences of their skill. They were here and in Spain for seven hundred years and you will see a typical Muslim Mosque. They also had a highly developed irrigation system which we still use,' Juan del Riego explained.

As they approached the town which, Penny thought, was little more than a big village, she could see far ahead in the flat country, and the mosque was the first thing they saw, a massive, impressive building with its red and white columns and arches as well as the amazingly beautiful ornamentation of the marble.

'The peasants on the island are a mysterious people in many ways, yet if treated justly and they can see it, they are loyal and good workers. I am fortunate because my five years here, when Pedro was ill, gave them confidence in me and they accept me. This means that many of our problems are quickly solved.'

As they went through the town they saw donkeys, some with boys on their backs and two water jars. The streets were narrow and the houses made of the same coloured stone as the boulders round the foot of the mountains that towered above them. The town was built on a higher plane than the flat country through which they had come and Juan del Riego explained:

'Sometimes we get very bad floods, so it is advisable to build above a certain level. The family houses, of course, are built on plateaux

30

in the mountains above us. Many were once small castles, guarding the island from intruders.'

There were cyclists and other carriages and carts, Penny saw, and from some of the open windows and the door of the tavern that was ajar came Spanish music. They also went past a large market where women crouched on the ground, selling fruit and flowers whose lovely brightness showed up vividly against the pale colour of the houses.

'It's beautiful,' Penny said slowly. It was so completely different from anything she had seen.

'It may look beautiful,' Juan del Riego said, his voice bitter, 'but the people who live on Vallora are far from beautiful.'

'I thought you liked them?' Penny was startled.

'The islanders, yes. My relations, no,' he said, his voice almost violent with hatred.

It startled her, so she turned to look at him and saw the thin hard line of his mouth, the way his thick dark eyebrows were drawn together, the fury in his eyes. Then why was he here? she wondered. Couldn't he have arranged for the children to learn English and engaged a good manager for the island as he was so rich? Was there some other reason for him staying here when he hated it and its inhabitants so much? Why did he hate them?

'Now we shall go across the range and see

31

the other town,' Juan del Riego said, changing the subject obviously. 'Most of our houses, as I said, are on the range.'

Slowly the carriage climbed the mountain-side, going through many unexpected flat plateaux. There were sheep, eating the sparse-looking grass, and many goats.

Despite the beauty and the sunshine, Penny was aware that the closer she got to their destination the more uncertain she became. What sort of man was this by her side? Surely it wasn't natural to hate your relations with such violence? And the cruel way he had spoken of the children's mother, implying that he was going to have things *his* way, regardless of anyone else's feelings.

Yet it was too late to do anything about it. She had taken the job and she must stay. Thanks be, she had a friend in Michael Trent, she thought, so at least if things got unbearable, he would help her. So she was not quite alone.

This comforted her as she looked round again, eager to miss none of the beauty. Far below them she could see small coves with light-coloured sand and waves racing in to pound against the huge boulders around. The bougainvilleas' long green arms seemed to have clasped everything within reach, so the beautiful purple flowers were everywhere, adding to the loveliness of the scene.

Now they were going slowly higher and she

could see white farmhouses far from the main road and reached by narrow tracks.

'Most of the big houses are on the other side of the mountains,' Juan del Riego explained. 'First we are going through the ravine to see the other town. It is still *siesta* time, so the Señora Magdalena Dominguez will be resting,' he said, his voice sarcastic as if suggesting that the Señora never did anything but rest!

The horses slowed down as they approached a high white wall over which yellow and red flowers crawled. They went through an archway. Penny caught her breath as she found they were crossing a narrow bridge high above a ravine where the ground was so far down below, it was hard to see it. For a moment she was really scared, and glanced at the man by her side. Why had they come this way? Was he going to push her over the low shelf that was on either side of the bridge? Could he then say she had fallen—or perhaps jumped?

How her father would have teased her, she thought, for her vivid imagination! They were nearly over the bridge that stretched across space because the lofty plateau had been cut in two by the chasm. It was a delicate-looking bridge built in two graceful arches, one above the other.

'This is known as Suicide Bridge,' Juan del Riego said with a strange smile.

33

The fear in her returned as she stared at him and he nodded:

'It is tragic that so many young people despair and die to escape the rigid discipline they are expected to accept.' A cloud seemed to cover his face, for it darkened, his eyebrows meeting, his mouth angry with suppressed fury. 'I nearly did, once,' he added.

'You did?' Penny echoed, amazed and shocked. '*You* did?'

He looked at her, his eyes narrowed. 'I was very young. If that is an excuse,' he said, shrugging his shoulders, then he turned away to shout up to the driver, something in Spanish Penny could not understand.

Then the Señor leaned back in the carriage and looked at Penny.

'You see the island is beautiful. It is in many ways, but in other ways it is evil. The islanders will not face the truth, they will only live in the past. But one cannot do that for generation after generation. They must realise that today is not yesterday and life has changed. It is impossible to live in the past. Naturally the young people have to go to the mainland as there is no school for older children here. They make friends, they learn about other lives and what is allowed and what forbidden. They return and rebel and then there is trouble.'

'Did you rebel?' Penny asked, then wished she hadn't, for his face grew dark with anger

34

again as he looked at her.

'Unfortunately I didn't. That is where I made the mistake of my life.'

CHAPTER THREE

Juan del Riego looked at Penny with amusement. 'You are afraid?' he asked.

She felt the colour rise in her cheeks. 'I was,' she confessed. 'The ground looked so very far away and . . . and if the carriage overturned . . .'

'It has never happened in all the years,' he said reassuringly. 'Or did you wonder if I would push you over the edge?'

Startled, she stared at him, for it was as if he was able to read her thoughts. Her cheeks seemed to be on fire as she looked at him, because he was laughing. His great boisterous laugh made the man in front turn in surprise and he laughed as well.

'You did!' Juan del Riego said at last when he could stop laughing. 'I saw the fear in your eyes. Do you honestly think I would murder you?' His face changed to anger. 'Has someone been talking to you?'

'Of course not! I . . . I'm sorry, but . . .' She took a deep breath. She had apologised, so that should be the end of it. 'It's just that I hate heights,' she explained.

He nodded. 'Many people do. Do not fear, we will not let you go alone where there is anything that could hurt you. Why are you afraid of me?'

It was another of his unexpected questions that left her with little or no time in which to think of an answer.

'I'm not afraid of you.'

'You were, then. Admit the truth. As we crossed the bridge you were afraid of me. Why? It is a simple question and I wish for a simple answer.' His voice had changed, become arrogant and impatient, and his hand closed round her wrist, his fingers digging into her flesh. 'The truth, please.'

The truth? Penny lifted her small pointed chin and stared at him.

'I . . .' she began, and paused as she tried to find the right words. 'I'm not really afraid of *you*. I think it was the terrible long drop down to the ground and the small ledge and . . .'

'And me? What have I said or done to make you believe I could be a murderer?' There was a threatening note in his voice.

'It's just . . . just my imagination. My parents always teased me about it. They said I ought to write books, because I'm so melodramatic and . . .'

'You have not answered my question.' His fingers dug painfully into the flesh of her wrist.

'It was . . . it was your hatred of Señora Dominguez. It wasn't like you, somehow. I mean, that kind of . . . of vicious hatred.'

'In other words, it would not surprise you should I murder Magdalena?' he asked.

'Of course not! Look, I mean you wouldn't.

I admit I was frightened. But it wasn't you—it was the height that frightened me.'

'You wondered if I should suddenly push you over the edge? Now why should I? Or are you suggesting that I am likely to murder you?'

Her cheeks burned. This was no way to start with your employer.

'I'm sorry—I did think how easy it would be to push someone over the edge. It wasn't you—as a person,' she faltered, hoping he would not recognize it as the lie it was. 'Look, I'm sorry if I offended you.' Her voice rose impatiently. 'I've said I'm sorry, so couldn't we leave it at that? I mean . . .'

He let go of her wrist and sat back. 'I know what you mean. A little joke has been carried too far.' He waved his hand. 'See how different the island can be—it is the same with the family.'

Penny looked round, glad that the embarrassing questioning was over. How could she have thought, even for a moment, that he might murder her? What could have made the thought come into her mind? And how was it he was so disconcertingly able to read her thoughts?

The countryside was strange now as the road led down the mountainside—for on one hand it was the beautiful greenness of everything and the vivid colour of flowers, but on the other it was black—black lava, no trees, nothing except the ground covered with lava, evidence of the day when there was a volcanic eruption.

'That happened two centuries ago. Maybe one day it will happen again,' Juan del Riego said.

'I hope not,' said Penny, looking at the ominous lava that covered everything it could, thus destroying it.

The second town was smaller than the first yet similar in other ways. As they drove through, people lifted their hats with a smile, the women looking at Señor del Riego quickly and giving what looked like a little curtsey before looking away again.

A silence had fallen between Juan del Riego and Penny, a strange silence that seemed to be strained. Was he angry with her and hiding it because she had accused him of hating his cousin's wife? Yet it was so obvious that he did.

They were driven down to the sea—a long sea-front where men were mending nets and small boats bobbed up and down in the little harbour and, looking over them, they could see the blue Mediterranean and also the cloudless sky. It was indeed beautiful.

Back up across the mountain range they climbed, the horses taking it placidly as if used to such work, Penny listening while Juan del Riego pointed out the houses of 'the family'. She felt quite confused with their names: Señor Rodriguez Alfonso Melado . . . Doña

Justina . . . there were so many she gave up trying to remember who they were, and looked instead at the huge castle-like houses that were hidden by the tall flowering bushes and trees so that she only got glimpses of the strange buildings—some were square, like children's bricks, others were turrets joined together by endless corridors.

'We are nearly at my cousin's home now,' Juan del Riego said slowly, his voice bitter. 'A house to be ashamed of, but she would have no alterations.'

Penny was quite unprepared for what she saw as the carriage left the main road and the horses trotted down the long avenue of tall eucalyptus trees. She caught her breath as they came out into the open and the house was hidden by a tall white wall with its wrought iron gates slowly opening as a man saw the carriage coming.

Once inside, they could see the house—more like a castle than anything, with a castellated roof and long chimneys, a wide balcony supported by the tall pillars that decorated the terraces outside the French windows. There was a stately courtyard with a fountain perched on four small white lions.

How still it is, was Penny's first reaction. No one working in the flower-filled garden—no dogs racing to greet them—no child, even. Indeed no life at all.

They walked towards the huge oak front

door with its enormous brass knocker. 'It's most unusual,' Penny said, trying to break the uncomfortable silence.

'Unusual is a good word,' Juan del Riego said bitterly. 'You should see my home. A million times more beautiful than this—also far more sensibly built.'

Again she found herself wondering why he had given up his own life simply because his cousin asked him to do so. Couldn't some arrangement have been made?

They knocked and a tall, swarthy, elderly man in white uniform let them in. He bowed stiffly to Juan del Riego but completely ignored Penny. It was so obvious—a deliberately planned insult—and Juan del Riego spoke sharply in Spanish to the butler before turning to Penny.

'This is José. He has been here since he was a boy. Any stranger to him is an enemy.'

'But why ?'

Juan del Riego shrugged his shoulders. 'He is afraid his life will be threatened. There are many peasants who have inherited fear from their ancestors, the families passing down the stories so that the children grow up, convinced that strangers may kill them.'

'But that's ridiculous, surely? I mean in this day and age . . .'

He smiled, a strange smile that had no amusement in it.

'This day and age? I told you that they live

in the past. Centuries in the past, in fact. They don't want to live in this age.'

They had gone into the hall as he spoke, an enormous hall, two storeys high with a huge glass dome as a ceiling and three curved staircases: at the foot of each there stood an armoured soldier, his face hidden by the steel mask.

Penny shivered. It wasn't the cold so much as the quietness. Not a sound was there to be heard.

Juan del Riego was talking to José and then turned to Penny.

'Her ladyship,' he said, his voice sarcastic, 'will now see us. How very kind of her!'

Impulsively Penny turned to him. 'Why do you hate her so?'

He smiled, a thin cold smile. 'I have reason to—you will understand when you get to know her.'

José led the way as they walked down the long cold hall and he opened a door, standing back politely but still not looking at Penny.

There was the warmth and brightness of the sunshine to welcome them as they went into the long lofty room—but that was all, for the place was otherwise very drab and dull. The French windows were open to a wide terrace. Seated in an armchair—looking rather like a throne—was the woman Juan del Riego hated so much.

She was beautiful—in a way, an out-of-date

way, Penny thought, as she stared at the dark silky hair elaborately done up, held in place by large diamond-studded combs. Señora Magdalena Dominguez was well made up but in a way Penny knew her father would have called 'chocolate-box prettiness'. It was unnatural—the pale pink skin clashed with the black hair, dark eyes and sulky mouth.

As they walked the length of the long room, the Señora watched them silently. An unfriendly atmosphere, Penny thought as she looked round her. The furniture was old. Not valuable antiques but just old with shabby armchairs and couches. The walls and curtains were a dull grey.

'I trust we have not shortened your *siesta*, Magdalena,' Juan del Riego said sarcastically.

Magdalena Dominguez looked at him. Penny shivered, for she had never seen such hatred in anyone's eyes before. Magdalena spoke in Spanish and then Juan del Riego introduced them to one another.

'This is Miss Penelope Trecannon.'

Señora Magdalena Dominguez bowed slightly. 'How do you do.'

'You *can* speak English?' Penny said impulsively, so relieved was she that someone else on the island could speak English as well as Michael Trent.

'I was well educated,' Señora Dominguez said stiffly. ' I can speak the language, though I dislike it. You speak Spanish? A little,

43

perhaps?'

Juan del Riego spoke before Penny could. 'She knows no Spanish at all. I had to find someone like her, as it is the only way. Now the children will *have* to learn, and they will do so more quickly if Miss Trecannon is unable to speak their language.'

'You think they will? You were always an optimist,' Señora Dominguez said sarcastically. 'Now, I suggest you allow me to have a short talk with Miss Trecannon, but I have no doubt she would like to rest. I think it would be best for her to meet the children in the morning.'

'A good idea for once,' he said briskly, and drew up a chair for Penny. 'I will see you also in the morning and introduce you to the children.' Then he turned to Señora Dominguez and smiled: 'I may be an optimist, but I usually get what I desire.'

'Usually, but not always,' Magdalena Dominguez said.

His face clouded for a moment, but then he smiled. 'How many of us get everything we want? It is, maybe, not good always to get what one wants.'

Penny shivered—this sort of hatred was something she had never met before. It was almost a relief when Juan del Riego went out of the room, yet, at the same time, she felt she was being deserted, left to face a danger she had never known before. Perhaps she was being melodramatic, as her father would have

44

said, yet she felt uncomfortable, ill at ease, even a little worried as to what would happen next.

It proved completely different from what she had expected, Penny was thinking half an hour later as she followed a tall sullen maid up the back flight of stairs and along the corridor. Maria was a tall elderly woman in a long dark dress and a starched white apron and a small cap perched perilously on top of her black hair. She hardly looked at Penny as she led the way.

It was a strange house—long corridors with uneven floors so that here and there were steps, down which, if you were not careful, you could fall easily. Baize-covered doors had to be opened and always they closed with a click. It was quite a relief when she was shown into her bedroom, where her luggage was waiting for her, and the maid took her to see the bathroom and left her.

Everything was quiet. Uncannily quiet, Penny thought, as she unpacked and put her clothes away before having a bath. As she lay in the delightfully hot water, the sun blazing through the open window, she thought of the past half hour when she had talked with Señora Dominguez.

At first she had asked questions about Penny's education, training and experience. Also how she had met Juan del Riego—and how had she got the job? She did not seem impressed by Penny's answers, in fact she admitted she could not understand why Penny, with no experience of teaching children, should get such a job.

'But I am not supposed to teach anything, *señora,*' Penny had said. 'Only to speak English to them.'

It was then Magdalena who talked— bitterly, angrily, even desperately. The strange things she had said, the accusations she had made. Was it possible that they were true? That Juan del Riego . . .

Penny got out of the bath and dried herself, putting on a white dress with a skirt that reached her knees. It was absurd—but then if the family were going to be so difficult, maybe Señor Juan was right and she should do as the Romans do. She sat in her bedroom, wondering what she was supposed to do next. She was sure she would get hopelessly lost in the winding corridors and end up somewhere she shouldn't! Where was she supposed to go to eat? Definitely not with the Señora Dominguez—she was far too posh to dine with a young governess—for that was what she insisted on calling Penny. Penny went to the window and some of her depression lifted as she gazed at the beauty before her. Sunset was coming and the sky changing colour—deep pinks, palest blue with a streak of green, and the red sun slowly dropping out of sight. The house was so high up on the plateau that she could see the waterfalls and the small coves, half hidden by the palm trees.

Again she wondered what to do. Was she expected downstairs—yet Señora Dominguez had said: 'I will see you in the morning.' Surely that was answer enough?

A better answer came later when her dinner was brought in on a tray. Afterwards Penny went to bed reading a paperback she had brought with her, trying not to think of her father or wishing he could come into her room to say goodnight—just as he had always done.

In the morning, breakfast came on a tray, so Penny ate it quickly, washed, and brushed her long red hair back, tying it loosely with a green ribbon. She put on a very little make-up, certainly nothing like she would have used in England.

Then she hesitated . . . should she go and try and find the Señora? Luckily the maid came and Penny followed her along the winding corridors and nearly stumbled several times as she failed to notice the steps and at last a door was opened and the maid stood back with a little bob but avoiding looking at Penny.

Penny gasped as she looked at the room. It was the kind you saw when conducted round an English stately home—huge paintings on the walls—an enormous bed with four poles and a decorated roof, with curtains hung down, half drawn round the four-poster. Señora Dominguez smiled.

'Come in. I trust you slept well.'

'Very well, thank you.'

How different the Señora looked! Her skin was sallow, her eyes had dark shadows under them, her hair was tied up in little ringlets by white ribbons.

'I am glad. A good night's rest is essential. Children are not easy to control—and definitely harder when you cannot speak their language. I am afraid you will find it very difficult.'

'I'll do my best,' said Penny, knowing that what had been said was true. It wasn't going to be easy at all.

The door opened and Penny turned quickly. Three children came in slowly, almost reluctantly. Their faces were pale and their eyes wide with what looked like fear.

Señora Dominguez held out her arms. 'Come to me, my darling children,' she said, then laughed. 'How can they understand?' she said to Penny, and spoke to them in Spanish.

The children stood huddled together at the door, and as their mother spoke, they moved forward slowly. The eldest was a girl— surprisingly blonde, for the others were so dark—she seemed to stand out with her honey-coloured hair and blue eyes. She guided the toddler, who began to scream so that the girl had to lift him to carry him to the bedside. The other child, a girl, was dark-haired.

The door opened again and this time it was

Juan del Riego and he spoke angrily:

'I said *I* would introduce her to the children!' He looked at the children and spoke in Spanish, and the children turned to him eagerly. He took the hands of the toddler and small girl and, ignoring Magdalena, spoke to the older girl and led the way out of the room.

He took them to the nursery, a big room with what were obviously new toys. A rocking horse—dolls, a doll's house . . . all the toys a child needs but that had only recently been given them, Penny noted as she saw the newness of them all. Was that Juan del Riego's doing? The way the Señora had spoken of him . . . she shivered as she remembered.

The eldest child leaned against him as he sat down, the toddler on his knees. 'This is Catalina, seven years old. She is a clever little girl, but at times she seems to retreat into herself as if frightened. The small girl is Techa. She is five and can be very tiresome, gets frightened easily and just screams. This toddler . . .' Juan del Riego went on, patting the toddler's head, 'is Abilio, not quite two and also easily scared.'

He spoke to the children next, in Spanish. Penny watched their faces. She saw the fear on Techa's face, the temper in little Abilio's as he struggled to get off his uncle's lap. Catalina's face was absolutely blank as she listened, her eyes fixed on the floor.

As Juan del Riego stopped, Catalina asked

49

a question in Spanish.

'She wants to know your name. "Miss Trecannon" isn't going to be easy to say.'

'I'd like them to call me Penny. After all, I'm going to be a friend, not a teacher.'

'Penny . . .' he said the word slowly, turning it round in his mouth as he repeated it: 'Penny,' making it sound like something revolting. 'It is a name without dignity. How can a child respect you when he calls you that?'

She felt her cheeks going hot. 'No one has ever said that to me before. I like the word Penny, far better than Penelope. They wouldn't be able to say that, I'm sure.'

'Let us think. Señorita . . .? no, I wish them to go away from any Spanish. Miss . . .? they could call you Miss.'

'I'd hate it,' Penny said quickly. 'Miss . . .! I want to be their friend, Señor del Riego,' she said, thinking it sounded rather pompous, since she rarely called him by name.

'*Penny*,' he repeated, looking amused. 'Have you always been called that?'

'Yes, always. And why not? Mother's grandmother was called Penelope and she was thrilled when I was born, so my mother decided to call me Penelope, but when the doctor saw me after I was born—I was a funny little thing—he said what a name for the poor child, so they always called me Penny. I can't see anything wrong in it,' she finished, irritated by his amused smile.

'There is nothing wrong. No, I agree. It is all right for a schoolgirl or a child, but a young lady . . .' The way he said the last two words was, to Penny, an insult, but she realised they could go on like this for ever, getting nowhere, and making the children stare at them as if puzzled and definitely frightened. So she turned to the eldest child and held out her hand. 'Catalina, I am Penny. Pen-nee . . .'

A little smile raced over the child's face. 'Pen . . . nee,' she repeated, and giggled. 'Pen-nee . . . Pen-nee.'

Juan del Riego smiled. 'I am afraid her mother will not approve. She will say it is impertinence for one so young to speak to . . .'

'One so old in such a way,' Penny finished for him. 'Look, I want to be friends with them, to be someone to play with, not someone strict and cross, and . . . and . . . and I want to do away with the generation gap. They look so scared, poor little things, and I don't want them to be scared of me.' She paused, but he did not speak, merely looked at her with those strange questioning eyes of his, so she went on: 'It isn't going to be easy for me, as you keep telling me. I can see just how hard it will be, as the children are scared to death. Somehow I've got to break that down. An easy word like "Penny" is a much better start.'

'You have a point there,' he said slowly. 'You have come prepared, I take it? You have some method?'

'Yes. A friend of mine is a teacher. She told me what to do. I've brought pictures and crayons . . .'

'That is good.' Señor del Riego stood up, putting the small boy on the ground. 'I can see you have everything planned.' He looked round the large nursery. 'Lunch will be served in here. If you have trouble with the children, tell José to fetch me. I am having a part of the garden wired off for the children, also a sand-pit and small swimming pool. You can, of course, swim?'

'Of course,' Penny said with a smile. So she had won for once! And the children could call her Penny. 'They've got some lovely toys—all new.' There was a question in her voice and he nodded.

'Yes. I remember when I was very young and my mother bought me a rocking-horse. I was so happy. Maybe that was why I was so interested in horses. My cousin Pedro was too ill to understand the children's needs. Their mother did not care.'

'But you care,' Penny said, her voice soft.

He looked startled. 'Of course I care,' he said crossly, and made his way to the door. 'Good luck, Penny. You'll need it,' he added with a strange smile as he closed the door and she was left alone with the children.

Smiling at them, not sure how to begin, she remembered the way Señora Magdalena

Dominguez had spoken the day before: 'My husband loved me so much. Juan, he was jealous. He had never liked me. My Pedro, it could never have been his wish that Juan should be a guardian of the children, for I am here, young, healthy, and their mother. Juan is a bachelor. What can he know of a child? Nor would Pedro, had he been in good health, leave the management of Vallora in Juan's hands. Pedro was like me. He loved the island as it is. Juan is not a Spaniard. He does not understand. He is cruel and callous. He has no warmth. He has never married, but he has broken many hearts. He could not care. All he thinks of is money. Though he has so much money, he wants more. I can only think that when my poor Pedro was so ill, Juan made him sign some papers and Pedro knew not what they were. I am afraid for the future. He will make the children confused. How can they go to an English school . . . and leave me?' Her voice had trailed away sadly as she touched her eyes with an embroidered handkerchief. 'My own children—not his . . .'

The door opened suddenly, startling Penny. She looked up and it was Juan del Riego himself, staring at her.

'You are lost in a fantasy world,' he said. 'I waited to hear you speak to the children, but you have said not one word. Why is it? Are you dreaming of Michael?'

'Michael?' Penny shook her head so that her

long red hair swung.

'Michael Trent. You . . .'

'Oh, Michael Trent. The one I met on the plane?' Penny laughed: 'No, I wasn't thinking of him. Actually—' she looked at him defiantly, 'I was thinking of you.'

'Of me?' He sounded amused. He leaned against the door, folding his arms. 'I am flattered. And what exactly do you think of me?' She hesitated and he smiled. 'I want only the truth.'

'Well, I was wondering why . . .' She drew a long deep breath and faced him. He might be used to throwing his weight around, having people bow and do what he told them, but he wasn't going to bully her. 'I wondered why, if you have a lovely home in South America and . . . and lots of money, why did you come here, giving up everything just for . . .'

'Money?' He nodded. 'I can see the once beautiful Magdalena has been talking to you. Of course you believed her. She is an excellent actress. I came because Pedro begged me to do so. He loved his children and was afraid for their future. He wished to sell the lease of the island, to take them away from this narrow bitter world. Long ago he wished to do this, but Magdalena objected and he was too weak with illness to fight her. He told me in his will that if the finances of the island prove to be as bad as he feared—he believed there is what is known as hanky-panky going on—then I am to

54

sell the lease. That is why I hired Michael Trent. Magdalena is happy here and she has other plans. Plans that I will fight in order to help these children.' His face was dark with anger, his eyes sparkling, his thick brows drawn together.

Penny looked at the children. They were all staring at him, but some of their fear seemed to have gone. Was he in the habit of losing his temper and were they so used to it, they were not afraid?

He turned and opened the door. 'I would have thought you had more sense than to believe what she told you—surely you should wait and discover the truth for yourself,' he said as he left the room.

CHAPTER FOUR

As the door closed, Penny was suddenly conscious of a desire to run after the Señor and tell him she knew it was no good—that when children look so frightened of you, what hope have you of making friends?

Not sure how to start, she wandered round the big white-walled nursery, stroking the rocking-horse, peeping into the dolls' house that looked as if no one had ever played with it, cuddling one of the dolls.

The children had not moved. Catalina's arm was round her small brother, little Techa was pale and her eyes were filled with fear. Penny sat down and smiled at them. She pointed her finger to herself.

'Pen-nee . . .' she said slowly. 'Pen-nee.' Then she pointed her finger at the little boy. 'You are Abilio.' She turned to Techa, pointing to her with a smile. 'Techa. Then . . .' she began, turning towards Catalina, but Techa was suddenly screaming at the top of her voice and so was Abilio. As their shrill frightened screams burst out, the door was flung open and two Spanish women hurried into the room, almost as if they had been waiting outside for this to happen. One was obviously a nanny, in a dark blue dress that nearly reached her ankles and a white starched apron and cap—the other a governess in a demurely grey suit who took Techa in her arms while the nanny took Abilio.

Both women looked angrily at Penny and spoke loudly, crossly, but in Spanish. Then they turned and hurried out of the room, slamming the door.

Penny didn't know what to do. She couldn't just let the children go like that—in any case, Catalina was with her, so Penny turned to the young girl.

'I wish I could speak Spanish, Catalina,' she said, suddenly near tears. How was she going to teach them to speak English when they were so frightened? 'Catalina . . .' Penny said very quietly. 'This is table . . . ta-bull . . .' she repeated slowly, touching the table in the middle of the room.

The small blonde-haired girl touched the table. 'Tay-bull . . .' she echoed.

Penny smiled and nodded. 'Good. Table . . . table . . . table,' she sang.

A smile flickered across the little girl's stony face and Catalina nodded, also singing, 'Tay-bull . . . taybull . . .'

The door opened and Señora Dominguez stood there. 'What is happening, Miss Trecannon?' she asked, her voice impatient. 'I thought you were to teach all the children, not only Catalina.'

'They screamed . . . and two women came in and took them away. Catalina stayed. She's a good girl . . .'

Señora Dominguez looked at Catalina and Penny saw the child's face change. It was as if she was retreating, closing herself in as she hung her head and said something in Spanish.

The Señora spoke sharply and turned to Penny. 'I apologise for what my daughter said of you. It was very rude indeed.' Then she laughed. 'I forgot—you speak no Spanish. She is bad. I must punish her. I was afraid this would happen. You cannot force children to learn something they hate and know that I hate it, too.' She caught hold of Catalina's hand and left the room, closing the door sharply.

Penny sat down. So now what? There was only one answer. Señor del Riego must be told!

Outside the nursery the house had regained its eerie quietness and as she hurried along the corridors, tripping several times down the unexpected and difficult-to-see steps, Penny finally found the staircase with its beautifully designed wrought iron banisters.

In the hall, she looked round worriedly. How could she find the Señor?

At the end was a double door of baize. It probably led to the staff's quarters, Penny thought, so made her way through it. She was right—there were several rooms with doors open that she could see were pantries and larders and a swing door that she opened. She stood dead in the doorway, shocked into stillness as the six women and four men at the long table looked at her.

Their dark swarthy faces were cold, their dark eyes full of hatred. There was a silence that could be felt. It seemed an endless time before José stood up. He said something in Spanish.

Penny shook her head. 'Señor del Riego . . .' she said slowly.

José seemed to understand, for he nodded and walked towards her, turning to speak to the others in a low but fierce voice. As he came closer—a tall, heavily built man glaring at her—she had the most absurd fears. Absurd, she called them afterwards, but at the time she was really frightened, for she had the stupidest feeling that José was going to strike her.

But of course he didn't. He murmured something as he passed her and led the way back through the double baize doors and into the hall, going to a door on the right and saying: 'Señor del Riego,' before he left her.

Penny knocked on the door. There was no answer, so she knocked again. Still no answer.

What was she to do? She walked down the hall to an open door and stood on the terrace, under one of the elaborately decorated archways. Deep yellow flowers hung their heads gracefully while the green stems clung tightly to the pillar. Ahead of her was the

59

garden. Penny stepped outside into the sunshine, looking up at the gorgeously blue sky, cloudless, and at the higher mountains behind the plateau, their rocks pushing up into the sky as if in search of something. The garden was gay with colour—red poinsettias, purple bougainvillea, white lilies. The trees were in flower—the white camellias sending out a fascinating perfume while the birds sang or darted down to the ground in search of food.

How beautiful it was, she thought. What a lovely place for a holiday. A holiday, yes, but not . . .

'And what do you think you are doing?' a deep vibrant voice asked.

Penny swung round. She had instantly recognised the voice. Who could mistake it? As so often, it was vibrant with anger.

'You're supposed to be with the children,' he began.

'I know,' she said, taking a step towards him. 'That's why I'm here. I knocked on your study door, but there was no answer, and I didn't know what to do.'

'You didn't know what to do?' he asked, his voice thick with sarcasm. 'What do you think I engaged you for? Not to stand basking in the sun, looking as if you were floating on a cloud, your face so radiant.'

She felt her cheeks go hot. If only they wouldn't!

'It is beautiful—' she retorted defiantly.

'Maybe, but that doesn't explain why you are here and not in the nursery.'

'I came to tell you . . .' she began, and told him that both Abilio and Techa had screamed and how the two women had come in and taken the children away. 'They were furious and shouted at me, but of course I couldn't understand. Catalina stayed with me and was good. We were singing the word *table* and touching the table when her mother came in . . .'

'And I imagine Catalina stopped singing and withdrew into herself.'

'You're right, she did. Her mother spoke to her in Spanish and Catalina said something and her mother apologised for the child's rudeness. She said she had said something unpleasant about me . . . then she took Catalina away, saying she would be punished.'

'You shouldn't have let them take the children. Why did you?' Juan del Riego asked impatiently.

'How can I stop a mother from taking her child? And the other children—they screamed terribly. They seemed terrified of me.'

'What had you done or said to them?'

Penny shrugged. 'What could I say? I patted the rocking-horse, looked in the dolls' house and hugged a doll. I don't think they've ever played with those things.'

'They haven't. Their mother won't allow

them to do so, but you must. I want them to learn to play—to enjoy life. Surely you are not such a coward as to be unable to stand up for the children?'

'I like that!' Something inside Penny snapped. He was being so unjust, not a bit sympathetic or helpful. 'What should I have done? Fought the nanny and the governess? Because they just grabbed the children and rushed off with them. And was I to knock down Catalina's mother and grab the child myself?' She stopped, so angry she couldn't speak, for Juan del Riego was smiling. 'It isn't funny, at all,' she snapped angrily, stamping her foot. 'Not in the least bit funny. Would your cousin have wanted the children to be in this . . . this mess-up? They can only be hurt . . .'

His laughter died instantly and anger darkened his face.

'I'll see that the children are not hurt,' he said angrily. 'Come with me.'

He walked into the house, up the stairs and down the corridor so fast that Penny had almost to run to keep up with his long strides. He opened a door and stood back a little to let her enter. She was rather breathless as she stared at Techa and Abilio playing on the floor with a teddy bear that must be nearly a hundred years old, Penny thought, judging by the shabby state it was in, with only one arm and one leg. Catalina was standing by the window. The governess and nanny were at the table playing cards. Both jumped up nervously when they saw the couple in the doorway.

Señor del Riego followed Penny inside and closed the door. He spoke to the children gently in Spanish, bending down to give Abilio a hug and pretending to pull Techa's long black hair. Then he looked at Catalina who was staring at him and Penny saw how the child's face changed—seemed to come unlocked and relaxed.

Then the Señor straightened and looked at the nurse and governess. His voice was quiet but thick with anger and Penny saw the two women getting more and more alarmed. Finally he turned away, opened the door and picked up Abilio. He spoke in Spanish and led the way, smiling at Penny as Catalina and Techa followed him.

Back in the day nursery, Señor del Riego played with the children, giving Techa and Abilio rides on the rocking-horse, bringing in an English word here and there and including Penny in the games.

'They loved their father dearly,' he told her. 'I have told them their father would love them more if they could speak English, that you are a friend and will not hurt them. I will stay with you for a few days so that they accept you . . .'

Penny was amazed. 'But how good of you,' she said impulsively. 'That would be a real help—but can you spare the time?'

'I am more concerned with the children's happiness and welfare than the state of the island. Actually I have two good men working for me whom I can trust. You must not worry when Techa screams. This is something she has done since she was a baby, and it is time she realised that screaming gets her nowhere. Abilio copies her, of course. I have told the nurse and the governess that they are not to interfere, that even if the children scream, they are not to come in. If they do,' his voice turned to something like ice, 'they will go. So if when I am out of the room, they try to take the children, you have the right to stop them, to refuse to let the children go. I do not think they will bother you.'

Penny could not get over it, that this callous, cruel man would devote time to help her with the children, but he did. He even ate lunch with them, making Techa and Catalina laugh at his jokes, even making little Abilio laugh with joy.

Afterwards the children went to the night nursery for the *siesta*. 'It is the habit here of resting for several hours in the afternoon. You would wish to do it?' Señor del Riego asked Penny.

She frowned. 'What? Waste two hours of this gorgeous sunshine?' she asked him. 'I'd rather wander round the garden and sit in the sun. I've some letters to write and . . .'

'That is good. It always seems a waste of

time to me. I'll show you round. At three o'clock, collect the children for more play and English. Tonight you will dine with us. We always dress up.' He gave an odd smile. 'I trust that you listened to my advice on clothes.' He looked at her, his eyes seeming to skim down her body, and he surveyed her rather demure white dress.

Penny smiled. 'Yes, I have.'

'Good.' He led the way down the corridor and the stairs, and several times Penny nearly missed the steps that were here and there and so hard to see in the gloomy corridors.

Outside they stood on the terrace, then walked through the garden where roses bloomed, such beautiful rose-red and yellow flowers with their delightful scent, and the broad herbaceous borders. How her father would love to see this, Penny was thinking, for that was what he had missed most when they moved to the flat after her mother's death. He had always had a garden until then. Maybe he and Fiona would buy a house. Penny often wondered how long Fiona would be happy in that small flat. She was a teacher, generally of disabled children, but Penny's father was a freelance journalist, often at home, and he had said he liked his wife to be there to welcome him, so he didn't want her to work!

Walking in the sunshine across the beautifully green grass, looking up at the mountains and down at the blue Mediterranean seemed to Penny to be like a fantastic dream. So much beauty . . .

Juan del Riego took her to the edge of the plateau, holding her arm, in case—he said with a smile—the height made her dizzy.

It was rather a frightening moment as she stood on the flat stone looking down through a narrow ravine at the sea. There was a promontory of land jutting out into the water and at the end was a small lighthouse. The waves splashed against the stones, tossing up white bubbles of surf.

'It looks small, but it has saved many lives,' the Señor said thoughtfully. 'In the past, you know, this island was renowned for its clever pirates. They would bring back their spoils and be sunk on this corner. Often there is a heavy mist down there and with that bit of land jutting out like a hungry tooth, many of the ships were sunk.

'The treasure was found?'

'Most of it. All of it, I'd say, though some may still think there are a lot of gold and silver coins sunk deep in the sand under too many feet of water. No one should ever swim in that cove, there is a dangerous current that is hard to fight.'

He turned back and they walked across the grass again towards a long white building. 'This is where the offices are. In Pedro's time, it was a shambles. That's what we're trying to put straight.'

He took her through the open door of one of the offices. A man of about Penny's age stood up at once.' He was a real Spaniard, Penny thought as she smiled at him when they were introduced.

'Valentin Taza, our chief clerk,' Juan del Riego said. 'He is a good worker, a man I can trust.'

Valentin had dark gentle eyes, a shy smile, thick black hair, and dark brows that met and a darkish skin. Now he looked shy, but his eyes told Penny that he found her attractive— perhaps even more than that. He spoke English, but slowly and with many apologies.

Juan del Riego then took Penny to the next office. There Michael Trent jumped up to greet them, his hand warm and firm as he took Penny's hand in his.

'How's it going?' he asked, and smiled at his employer. 'I told her it wouldn't be easy.'

'I told her that, too. You know what the local people are like, Trent, so you can imagine the difficulties, but we'll make it,' said Juan del Riego, his voice firm.

'We'll fight to the last ditch,' Mike said with a laugh.

Juan del Riego nodded. 'Exactly.' He turned to Penny. 'I want to show you the swimming pool, and then I have some phoning to do.'

How lovely the garden was, Penny thought, as she followed him down the paved path that led to the house. The pool was some way from the house with a hedge of flowering roses round it and several tall red and white sunshades stuck into the ground. The pool was in the shape of a heart.

It had no shallow end, Penny was told.

'The children must never be brought in this part of the garden. I am making a shallow safe pool to be near the sand pit.'

'That will be lovely for them.'

When they got back to the house, it was nearly three, so Penny hurried up to her bedroom. She had learned to notice certain pictures on the corridor's walls so that she could find her own room without difficulty. She brushed her hair and powdered her nose, thinking how Fiona would laugh if she could see her with so little make-up on. Was she being a coward? Penny wondered. Should she have given in to him about her clothes? Should she have worn what she liked? Yet he *was* her boss—and if the people of the island were narrow-minded, then . . .

She hurried along to the night nursery. A little nervously, she knocked and then opened the door. The room was empty. Puzzled, she went to the play nursery. That, too, was empty.

Not sure what to do, wondering if she should go down and tell him and start the trouble over again, Penny walked slowly up and down the corridor. A door opened and Señora Magdalena Dominguez came out of the room. She was wearing a long cream dress, embroidered with purple flowers. On her head was a tall silver comb from which her cream lace mantilla hung.

'You seek the children, Miss Trecannon?' she asked with a smile. 'They are waiting in the carriage for me. Today I take them to their great-aunt for a visit. We may be home late, so you shall have your dinner in your room—I have told José. Now you can rest, or lie in the sunshine, a luxury you do not often have in England.'

Not sure what to say—for how had she the right to stop the children's mother from taking them on a visit, yet the Señor . . . ? Penny went back to her room and sat outside on the balcony that ran right round the house. There was also a staircase that led down to the terrace. She would write to her father and to Fiona, too, telling them all about the Island, the gorgeous garden, the beautiful flowers, the lovely sunshine. All the good things, and there were many. She would say nothing about the hatred she felt—nor of the dark dreariness of the house—or of the difficulties she could see that lay ahead.

How, she asked herself, was she ever going to teach these children to speak English? Even though the Señor was being surprisingly helpful—at least where the children were concerned. What hope had *she* of succeeding?

CHAPTER FIVE

Penny had just started to eat her dinner in her bedroom when there was a resounding banging on the door which immediately opened as if the person banging on it was impatient.

Startled, Penny half rose as Señor del Riego stood in the doorway, his face dark with fury.

'I told you that you were to dine with us!' he declared, slamming the door to behind him and walking towards her. 'I give the orders and you obey them!'

She stood up. 'The Señora told me she was taking the children to see their great-aunt and they would not be back for dinner and . . . and I was to eat in my bedroom.'

'A likely story!'

'It's true!' Penny's anger began to grow. 'I'm not a slave—do you think you can order everyone around and . . .'

'I employ you . . .'

'You never let me forget it!'

'I said you were to dine with us and I mean it.' He moved his hand quickly and the tray shot off the small table, flew through the air, and landed in a splash on the floor as the plates broke into little pieces and the prawn salad was scattered round the room.

'Look at the mess!' Penny found it hard to

speak for a moment. 'Just look!'

He strode to the long purple cord hanging near the window and pulled it sharply. 'It will be cleared up, and you will change into something more suitable for dinner. You have exactly twenty minutes, and I shall expect you in the drawing room where we are having drinks.' He paused, some of the anger having left his face as if the violent movement had released some of his fury. 'I tell you,' he went on, lifting his hand and shaking a finger at her, 'that if you do not come down, I shall come and fetch you and carry you downstairs, no matter how much or how little clothing you are wearing . . .' His mouth twitched as if he was trying not to smile.

'It isn't funny,' Penny told him, holding the back of her chair so tightly she could see the whiteness of her knuckles caused by her tension. 'Why must I come down?'

'For the simple reason that I want to help you.' He stood, his arms folded, towering above her. 'I will not allow you to be treated like a leper or a servant. You are not a governess but a companion, a friend of the family. Do you understand?'

She stared at him and saw the sincerity in his eyes. He was right—if she was to be isolated, treated as the Señora did treat her, the servants would despise her, not only with hatred but with contempt. That would make everything even harder than it was already.

71

There was a gentle knock on the door and he turned, saying something in Spanish. Maria, the tall sullen maid, came in. Her eyebrows lifted in surprise as she saw the mess on the floor. Juan del Riego spoke rapidly in Spanish and surprisingly her dark sullen face relaxed and broke into a smile. Marie nodded, gave Penny a quick look and hurried away.

'What did you say to her?' Penny asked.

'The truth. That I had been angry with you—my friend—and lost my temper. That she can well understand, for we with Spanish blood are apt to blow our tops.' He chuckled, a deep sound that was full of amusement. Then he held out his hand towards Penny. 'I apologise. It was unforgivable. Will you forgive me?' He looked so pathetic Penny found it hard not to laugh. She knew he was acting, but it was a friendly act, not one to make her feel small.

'Yes,' she said, 'I forgive you.'

He lifted her hand to his mouth and kissed it. Then he kissed her wrist and her arm to the elbow. She stood very still, not sure how to react. Was this a Spanish way of apologising?

He dropped her hand gently and stood back with a smile. 'You have only fifteen minutes now. Is it time enough?'

'I can manage,' she said with a smile.

'Good. I will be waiting and we will have a drink before we eat. I will see you as soon as you can manage.' He looked down at his dark suit, well-cut, elegantly modern with a white starched shirt and black tie. 'I must warn you that our women are dressed not only demurely but with dignity.'

'I will remember,' she said meekly, and he smiled at her and left the room.

She had to work fast. She looked at the wardrobe. How carefully she and Fiona had chosen the evening gowns she needed. Finally Penny chose a leaf-green dress, with a full skirt that whirled as she moved. She brushed her hair and twisted it up high on her head, thankful that she had brought out plenty of hair-clips. Then she made up carefully, thinking again how odd it was not to be able to use the make-up she would have done in England. One thing, she thought, she would see how the local females dressed. Maybe Juan del Riego was wrong, maybe he was the old-fashioned narrow-minded person he talked about so much.

Surveying herself in the mirror, she heard a gentle knock on the door and without thinking, said: 'Come in.'

There was another knock and she realised that whoever it was outside could not understand English, so she went to the door and opened it. A different servant was there, one much younger, with beautiful dark eyes full of curiosity and a quick smile as Penny smiled and indicated the mess on the floor. The girl gave a little curtsey and her eyes widened as she looked at Penny. Slowly the girl shook her head, her face breaking into a smile. Penny took it as meaning the girl liked the leaf-green dress.

Penny gave one last look at herself in the mirror, but she did not see what the others were to see: a lovely girl with a fair skin and green eyes, with red hair that would be a lovely colour in the light from the chandeliers, a girl with a slim body and a full, beautiful mouth. Made for kisses, more than one person was going to think.

Penny was a little nervous at what lay ahead, for it was quite possible that the Señora would be annoyed to see her, having told her to dine in her bedroom, yet knowing Señor del Riego would be there comforted Penny.

Along the corridor, holding up her long skirt as she carefully looked for the unexpected steps that seemed to try in vain to level the floor, she hurried down the beautiful staircase and into the hall where she paused.

Again the strange still silence struck her. It was as if she was alone in the big ungainly house, for that was what it was. A door opened and Juan del Riego stood there.

'Good,' he said with a smile. 'Full marks for a quick change. Come inside and meet some of the family.'

He held out his hand and took hers, leading her into the room as if he was leading some royal lady, Penny thought with a sudden

74

desire to giggle at his somewhat pompous melodramatic action. He smiled at her and she smiled back, startled by the reassurance it gave her.

She had not been in this room before and she looked round her quickly. Three huge chandeliers hung from the ceiling, filling the room with a harshly bright light. The furniture was just as old, just as shabby as in the other rooms. The walls were covered with huge portraits of what were obviously ancestors of the family, judging from the clothes they wore.

Señora Dominguez was sitting in a chair, leaning forward with a smile.

'I managed to get the children away from their great-aunt,' the Señora said in a friendly voice. 'She loves them so much she cannot bear to let them go. I am glad that we came back in time.'

A tall, heavily-built yet still lean man had come from where he had been standing by the window.

'Miss Trecannon,' Juan del Riego said formally. 'I wish to present my cousin, Señor Alfonso Rodriguez Melado.'

'This is my pleasure,' Señor Alfonso said as he bent and kissed Penny's hand. 'It is not often in this country that we have the delight of an English girl with such lovely fair skin and such beautiful hair.'

Penny felt herself blushing as she looked at him. He was amazingly handsome. An odd word to use, perhaps, yet he was completely unlike any man she had ever seen, with his olive skin, thick dark hair, growing somewhat long, dark eyes with a strange expression in them, and dark eyebrows. He had a quiet voice, very different from his cousin's angry vibrant tone.

Penny was led to a chair and given a glass of something or other. She drank it slowly while Alfonso sat by her side, leaning forward, his face absorbed as if by her words, his dark eyes travelling up and down as he looked at her, and asked questions as to what part of England she came from—saying how much he loved the country, how beautiful were the ladies. 'So different from ours—they have much more freedom,' he said, and there was a look in his eyes that for a moment frightened her, for she felt exactly as if he had ripped the clothes off her . . . which was absurd, as her father would have said.

The dinner was delectable—again Alfonso sat next to Penny while Juan del Riego talked to Pedro's widow, Magdalena. They were talking quietly but seriously in Spanish and it was obvious that both were controlling an anger that was liable to burst at any moment. Alfonso was interesting to talk to, so Penny really enjoyed the meal. Afterwards Alfonso insisted on taking her out into the garden to see the beauty of the moonlit sea.

It was beautiful—a pleasantly warm evening

with a round full moon in the star-splashed sky, the palm trees standing, silhouetted against the light, and the sea, far below, with a great swathe of brightness across it.

They were talking as they walked and Alfonso's hand was under her elbow, and it was with quite a shock that Penny realised they were now standing on the flat stone where earlier that day Juan del Riego had stood by her side.

It was dark down below, the ravine sides shutting out the moonlight, but the lighthouse stood out like a small gallant figure at the end of the piece of rock.

She felt Alfonso's fingers tighten round her arm and turned to look at him.

He was smiling at her, a strange smile that rather frightened her. Which was absurd, she reminded herself, for why should it? He was a man older than Juan, a sophisticated man with good manners, so why should she have this fear?

'It is quite a fall, is it not?' Alfonso asked, leaning forward so that she had to do the same and the fear grew greater and gripped her.

'I hate heights . . .' she gasped.

He stepped back at once. 'I am sorry, I had no idea,' he said apologetically. 'Many hate heights, but they do not alarm me at all. Let us walk back, or my cousin will think we have eloped together.' He laughed and Penny laughed, too, but she was very glad as they walked away from the frightening spot.

Back at the house, Magdalena Dominguez was playing the piano while Juan del Riego strode up and down the room, frowning a little as he saw Alfonso and Penny return.

'A most enjoyable walk,' Alfonso said slowly, his slight accent betraying the fact that he was Spanish—as if, Penny thought, his very look didn't tell you that. She had never been good about history, but she remembered seeing a painting once of some Spanish conquistadors and Alfonso had a perfect resemblance to them. She could also imagine him sailing in a boat, ready to attack, to steal, and to feel proud of what they had gained. 'I am afraid I must go now, after a most enjoyable evening.' He looked at his cousin, who didn't return the smile. 'The children are lucky to have such a charming companion. I am tempted myself to pretend I cannot speak English so that she might favour me with her company.' He bowed to them all, kissing the Señora Dominguez hand as well as Penny's. Juan del Riego walked with him to the door and Penny knew a moment of discomfort as Magdalena Dominguez began to play the piano again, ignoring Penny completely.

Taking it as a hint, Penny went to the hall as Señor del Riego returned.

'So—' he said as they stood in the cold hall. 'You have met my cousin. What do you think of him?'

Penny hesitated. What did she think of Alfonso? Behind her she could hear the music as Magdalena played the piano with an almost fierce force as if she was trying to show as well as get rid of the anger that possessed her.

'He is very handsome,' Penny said slowly.

'Is he?' Juan del Riego sounded amused. 'You are young, immature and obviously not accustomed to the society of sophisticated men. How did you get on in the garden? Did he make . . .'

'He was very polite and interesting to talk to,' Penny said quickly, aware that her cheeks were going red. 'We . . . we went and looked down at the little lighthouse.'

'You did? And you were afraid?' Juan del Riego asked, sounding amused.

'Yes—I hate heights, as you know.'

'Of course—then I would advise you not to go there when alone, either in the day or at night. Part of the stone is uneven, it is not difficult to trip over it . . .' He paused. 'It would be a long fall,' he said slowly and quietly.

Was he thinking what she had thought as she stood on the smooth rock and Alfonso's hand was on her arm? Was her instinct right and had Alfonso been thinking of pushing her over the edge? But why should he? He did not even know her. Or was he one of those mentally deranged sadists who delight in hurting people? Had he deliberately taken her there to see how she would react? Yet if he did

79

so, why?

'Yes. He was very apologetic when I said I was afraid of heights,' Penny said quickly, then wondered why she was on the defence of the man who had momentarily frightened her.

'He would be.'

She stared, puzzled, at the man by her side. 'You don't like him,' she said accusingly.

Juan del Riego smiled. 'Neither does he like me.'

'Then why ask him for dinner?'

'He asked himself—or else Señora Magdalena did. I leave the invitations to her, for she knows of all the family feuds and who will sit next to whom—and who will not be in the same room as someone else. You can have no idea of the hatred on this island—of the delicate walk one must make or else some great family feud will be dug up and tempers rise and perhaps there will be physical action . . .'

'Like knocking a tray off the table,' Penny said, then wondered if she should have said it, but he was not annoyed: he merely smiled.

'You are so right. Actually I would not say this of the ordinary Spaniard, but I am talking of the family on this island. Here is a small community who live, as I have told you many times, in the past and refuse to leave it. They delight in remembering what is past, they have little to do and nothing to talk about, so they dig up past stories and become determined to carry on feuds that should have been forgotten centuries ago. Why blame the people of today for what their ancestors did several centuries ago? It is ridiculous. Then they quote the sins of their fathers and all that. It makes me so angry. Today is here and tomorrow waits for us. We cannot waste time living in the past. Let it be forgotten.' He turned away, as if feeling he had said too much, and spoke over his shoulder. 'I trust you will have a good night. I will see you in the day nursery at nine o'clock.'

'Yes, goodnight.' Startled by the abrupt ending to their talk, Penny turned and went up the staircase, then remembered she was on the wrong one.

Once up in the corridors, it seemed to take ages before she found the painting that she recognised of a small boy standing by a tall white horse. It was well painted; on the boy's face was so much happiness it was moving just to look at it. His hand was on the horse. Maybe it was a present, something he had longed for and had just been given.

Her bedroom was just past the painting. She was glad the painting was so impressive, for it always caught her eye as she walked along the endless, uneven-floored corridors.

In her room, she hastily undressed and got into bed. How quiet everything was. Again, the feeling of being completely alone in the house filled her—which was absurd. But then so much of what she felt in this house was absurd.

It was all imagination, as her father would have said. Why had she been afraid as she stood high above the little lighthouse? Why was she afraid as she stood at the kitchen door and the servants had looked at her with such hatred? Had that been her imagination? Was that all it was?

*   *   *

In the morning she went to the day nursery early, taking the pictures of animals and cars and houses and ships she had brought with her, as well as the crayons. She laid these out on the table and put the chairs ready. Maybe, she thought, it was a mistake to point a finger at the children as she said their names? Maybe that was what had frightened them so much.

It was with some nervousness that she opened the door to let the children in. Both the nanny and the governess were with them, but they did not speak or even look at Penny. They said something in Spanish to the children, then left Penny alone with them.

She sat down at the table and Catalina took little Abilio by the hand and led him to look at the pictures. Techa's interest was also caught and Penny knew a moment of relief, for it looked as if she had started the right way.

Techa even picked up a crayon and tried it on the paper, drawing something and looking at Catalina eagerly. Penny slowly drew a cat with big whiskers and a waving tail. Catalina looked at it and at her.

'Cat . . . cat . . .' Penny said slowly.

The little blonde girl giggled. 'Cat . . . cat . . . cat,' she repeated, then said a Spanish word, looking at Penny.

Penny tried to say it and Catalina giggled again and repeated it, making Penny say the word until Catalina was satisfied. Penny wanted to laugh, but decided to take it seriously, though Señor del Riego would not approve, she felt sure. She wasn't there to learn Spanish but to teach English, and he would probably shout at her for disobeying him!

A knock on the door startled them all and Techa dropped the crayon. José, the butler, came in and with no expression on his face handed Penny an envelope. She thanked him and he left the room. Puzzled as to who the letter could be from, Penny went to the window, leaving the children to do what they liked, for that was the way she wanted it, that they should enjoy the lessons, not see them as something hard and frightening.

The letter had not come by post. The writing was large and dramatic. She opened the envelope. The letter was brief.

'Unfortunately I have been called to the mainland. I may be away several days but will return as soon as possible. Remember that I am your employer and that you must obey

83

my wishes.'

It was signed in thick sprawling handwriting that was—in the signature—hard to read. She turned to look at the children. Juan del Riego would be away for several days. How was she going to manage?

She said nothing but went back to the table, ignoring the children, who seemed to have found something to interest them. Little Abilio was clutching several crayons and drawing lines and circles on paper. Techa was slowly and deliberately drawing a man who was walking in the sea while Catalina was frowning as she looked at the pictures. Penny began to draw a ship, but she said nothing at all, feeling that maybe this would help them from being frightened.

They all jumped when the door was swung open and hit the wall as if it had been flung by an impatient hand.

It was Señora Dominguez. Instantly the children changed. Abilio began to scream and Techa cried, while Catalina went very pale, her eyes wide.

The Señora was smiling at Penny. 'Ah, I have heard that Juan has left the island. It is true?' She looked at the envelope on the table.

'Yes,' said Penny, shivering a little, for it was as if an icy wind had entered the room and she could not take her eyes from the children, who looked petrified with fear. Why? This was their mother.

'Ah, that is good. I knew that if I was patient, things would go my way.' Señora Dominguez was beautiful in a chocolate-box way, Penny thought, as she had when they first met. Now the Señora was looking triumphant. 'That is very good. Now we can stop this nonsense,' she said, sweeping her hand as if pointing to the toys with scorn. 'And you can enjoy yourself, Miss Trecannon. You can lie in the sunshine and become tanned. There are many handsome men on the island who would be delighted to enjoy your company and my poor children can enjoy life without that great bully using his whip,' she said bitterly, then clapped her hands sharply and instantly the nanny and the governess appeared, scooping up the smaller children and hurrying away, while Catalina followed them, her face blank.

'But, *señora*,' Penny said quickly, 'the Señor told me I was to . . .'

'Forget what he said. It is of no importance. He need not know, in any case,' Señora Dominguez said, smiling at Penny, and she turned and walked out, leaving the door ajar.

Penny hesitated. He had told her to obey him and not allow Señora Dominguez to have her way. But how was she to be stopped?

In despair, Penny hurried down to the ground floor, out into the garden, but this time she did not see the beauty of it, for she felt she had let Juan del Riego down. But what could she do? If only she knew!

CHAPTER SIX

It was four days before Señor del Riego returned to Vallora. Four nightmare days for Penny, as she was in a most difficult situation. She told the sympathetic Michael Trent when she ran downstairs and out into the garden after the children had gone and the Señora had talked to her.

'What can I do?' Penny had asked desperately. 'He tells me that he must be obeyed, but how can I take the children away from their mother?'

Valentin Taza, who had joined them, chuckled. 'Also you must do battle with the nurse and the governess. It is not possible.'

'The Señor seems to think it is,' Penny sighed. 'He'll be furious.'

'He does the impossible and expects us ordinary creatures to do the same,' Michael said, laughing. 'Frankly, Penny, I don't see what you can do about it. She is the children's mother.'

'I just can't understand it. I mean, she told me I could enjoy a holiday and that Señor del Riego need not be told . . .' Penny stopped, startled by the two men's laughter. 'Well, I mean that isn't right, is it?' she asked.

Michael had put his arm round her shoulders and hugged her. 'Bless you, you ethical little angel! Of course it isn't right, but how many things are one hundred per cent right? If I were you, Penny, I should accept the situation. You have far too many people against you, so you wouldn't have a hope. Why not enjoy yourself? Life in the sunshine . . .'

'But I've got nothing to do or read or . . .'

'You cannot just do nothing?' the good-looking Valentin asked with a smile, but Michael had understood.

'I'm going into town later today and you can come too and get some books and knitting and sewing,' he grinned.

'I see you know women,' Penny teased, feeling she was no longer alone.

'I had five sisters,' Michael told her. 'I know your sex well.'

He and Valentin had been good friends during the awful four days, taking her shopping, swimming in the pool with her, cheering her up as she needed it badly, for sometimes, sitting in her bedroom alone, she felt she had let her employer down. Surely there should have been some way in which she could have carried out Juan's orders?

It was a perfect day when he arrived back. Penny was lying by the pool in a swimming suit, a cotton hat pulled over her eyes because of the brightness of the sun. She was half asleep when his voice shook the ground around her—or seemed to with its violence.

'What the hell are you doing here? I told

87

you . . .' Señor del Riego demanded.

Penny blinked, pushing back her hat as she sat up. He was standing above her and she scrambled to her feet. She saw how angry he was, just as she had expected, and something seemed to snap inside her. After all, she had done her best.

'Waiting for you to come back,' she said quickly.

'Is that so? Hardly likely. I understand you have completely neglected the children, spending your time out here, leaving them alone, spending all your time with men— getting yourself a bad name. The very things I warned you about.'

'And you believe that?' The words seemed to leap out of her mouth, she was so angry. 'It's all lies. Five minutes after I got your note, she came in.' There was no need for Penny to say who 'she' was. 'She told me I could have a holiday, because it wasn't right for the children to learn English.' She stared at him. Was he believing her? 'She also said I needn't tell you about it at all.'

'And what did you do? Seize your opportunity to go out and enjoy yourself?' he asked sarcastically.

'What could I do? There were three of them, and I'm not used to violence,' she told him, and saw the little tremble of his mouth that told her he was trying not to smile. 'Look . . .' She took a deep breath, clenching her hands, digging her nails into the palms as she glared at him. 'I'm sick and tired of the way you expect me to do the impossible. Was I supposed to fight the nurse and governess—to hit your cousin's widow and drag the children to my room and lock them in?' Her voice rose shrilly, but she realised she was horribly near tears. 'You just don't understand because you don't want to!' She stamped her foot and wished she hadn't, because it was a childish thing to do. 'I had every meal in my bedroom. I haven't seen the Señora since that first day. I came down to ask Mike's advice and he agreed that there was nothing I could do . . .' She had to stop speaking, for her voice was trembling, and whatever happened, she must not cry.

'Excuse me,' Mike's English voice broke in, and Señor del Riego turned, frowning.

Mike and Valentin were both standing there. Valentin spoke quickly in Spanish, but Mike was obviously determined to speak, so he stepped forward.

'Valentin and I took Penny to do some shopping because she had nothing to do and no books to read.'

'Her job was to look after the children,' the Señor said angrily.

'It was impossible for her. They treat her without respect.' Mike sounded angry, too.

Juan del Riego frowned, but he also looked thoughtful. 'I will settle the matter,' he said, and walked off.

Mike gave Penny a hug. 'Don't look so miserable, Penny. He won't bite your head off.'

She smiled. 'I was so glad when you and Valentin turned up. I was so angry I thought I was going to cry.'

'I heard your voice—so unusually shrill. I got Valentin because I knew they'd have lied.'

'Do you think . . . do you think he'll . . .' Penny hesitated and Mike chuckled.

'Give you the sack? Not likely. That I'm sure of—eh, Val?'

Valentin was laughing. 'He would be mad to let you go. You are like the sunshine on a gloomy day.'

Penny laughed. 'Thanks for boosting my morale. Now what do I do?'

'Go indoors, have a shower and put on some clothing that is less . . . well,' Mike's eyes twinkled, for he knew about the Señor's views on the clothes she should wear, 'undignified, or should I say provocative?'

'And wait?'

'Keep in your room until he sends for you. There will be a great row—mostly noise, but it might frighten you,' Mike said with a smile, and winked at Valentin. 'You Spaniards!'

Valentin laughed. 'Better a good blast and then forget it than to let it curdle inside you while you keep a stiff upper lip, you English!'

'I wonder . . .' Penny said slowly. 'It may help the person who is shouting, but I think it's the other one who'll never forget the things

90

that have been said and will always be hurt.'

Mike whistled softly. 'We'd better watch out, Valentin. No quarrels with Penny or she'll never forgive us.'

'I didn't say that. I meant that if you have nasty things said to you, it's hard to *forget* them.'

'Though the person who's said it feels better?' Mike asked.

'Yes, that's what I mean. I think quarrelling is selfish—I hate it.'

'Poor you, then,' said Mike. 'You'll hear plenty of quarrels round here.'

'So it seems. Anyhow, thanks to both of you. You kept me going.'

Valentin bowed and laughed. ' 'Twas our pleasure, *señorita*, far more than yours.'

'I'll say that again, Penny,' grinned Mike.

As she collected her things and hurried to the house, she thought how lucky she was to have two such good friends, for the last four days would have been a nightmare without them. Even with them, it had been bad enough.

The house was as still and quiet as usual, so she hurried to her room, then hastily showered and put on a demure white linen dress, collected the pictures and crayons in case Señor del Riego sent for her as soon as he had settled everything.

The point was: how would he do that? It sounded so simple, but . . .

Actually it turned out far more simple than she would have dared hope. José arrived with a note, asking her to go down to the hall to wait for the carriage. They were going to fetch the children from Doña Justina Melado whom they were visiting.

Penny knew then why she had not heard a sound of the children or found them when she went to the day and night nurseries to look. She hurried to the hall, for something told her Señor del Riego must be in a flaming temper by now, but to her surprise he met her with a smile.

'Good,' he said. 'I thought you might still be at the pool.'

'I came in right away.'

'Good. You knew I'd settle it?'

As they walked out of the house, she looked up at him.

'Yes, I knew you would, but I just couldn't think how.'

He laughed. 'Simplicity itself. I told Magdalena that she either stopped this nonsense and let the children learn English or I would take them away to England myself.'

'You didn't?' Penny was shocked. 'You wouldn't—really?'

'I most certainly would.' Juan waited as the man in white uniform opened the carriage door so that he and Penny could climb in.

As the horses began to trot, Juan looked at the pretty girl by his side. 'You sounded horrified. Why?'

'She's their mother.'

'Physically yes, emotionally no. She doesn't give a damn for her children. But she wants to hang on to them. They are a weapon, you see.'

'A weapon?'

He nodded. 'If anything happened to me, then she would automatically become the children's guardian and therefore have access to their money, because they are afraid of her. Surely you can see that?'

'Well . . .' Penny hesitated. 'They do seem to alter when she comes into the room. Particularly Catalina.'

'Self-defence. That was how my cousin had to behave. Weak from illness, he hated quarrels and would often shock me by doing what she wanted. He didn't know, I realised later, just how ill he had been and his attitude was "anything for a quiet life". Also, of course, with the children she is in our family.' His voice was, for a moment, proud. 'Otherwise she is nothing.'

'But . . . but . . .'

He laughed. 'I agree. It's out of date, but on Vallora it is most important. She came from the mainland, so is not one of us.'

'Is Alfonso one of you?'

One of Juan's eyebrows lifted. 'You are interested? Yes, he is one of us. The great-aunt we are now visiting is his mother. It was Alfonso's father who was disinherited—

otherwise Alfonso would be in charge of the island.'

'Alfonso would?' She was startled.

'Yes—his father was supposed or said to have done something unforgivable. Unforgivable, I should say, in the eyes of the family. No doubt whatever he did would not be even thought of twice today. Alfonso's grandfather passed the lease over to Pedro's father when he knew he was dying. Alfonso has never forgiven his father or Pedro, yet can you think what a shambles this place would be with Alfonso in charge? I doubt if it would be his—he would have sold the lease by now—though . . .' Juan del Riego's voice changed, became less sure, more thoughtful, 'I have an idea—which may be wrong—but I think Alfonso believes, like many others, that there is treasure in the water round us. Souvenirs, one might call them, of the days when our ancestors were pirates. I think there is no hope, but there are some who will never accept the truth. If he had charge of the island, he could hunt for the treasure secretly and have all the results for himself. That, of course, is what he wants.'

The carriage was going slowly down a winding road towards the sea. 'Doña Justina Melado is an old lady and she has always been kind and loving to the children, disappointed I think because Alfonso has never married and she has no grandchildren.' Juan turned to look at Penny. 'You had a difficult time while I was

94

away?' His voice was gentle.

'It was awful. I felt so bad about it.' She looked up at him earnestly. 'Honestly, I tried everything. I couldn't find the children or . . . I mean it, I felt terribly bad about it. That I had let you down, but . . .'

'It was not your fault. I should have known what she would do. Unfortunately I was sent for in an emergency and had no time to make sure you would be protected from their hatred. You must have felt lonely.'

'Oh, I did, terribly. It was Mike and Valentin who were so kind.'

'Only kind?' Juan asked, his voice amused.

'They were more than kind. They were sympathetic. I felt so guilty—I mean, you employed me to look after the children and I hadn't . . .' Her voice was unsteady and suddenly Juan's hand was over hers. He lifted her hand and kissed it and smiled at her.

'Please stop having that guilt complex. You did all you could. I knew that Magdalena must be lying when she told me that.'

'Then why did you accuse me?'

'I accused you of nothing. I like to make you angry,' he said with a smile. 'You can have no idea how beautiful you are when angry.'

Penny was startled. 'Me? Beautiful?'

'And why not? Do you not ever look in a mirror? Your hair and your eyes and your skin, soft and beautiful as a peach. Then when you are cross, your eyes flash and you go bright

95

red—even your little nose goes red . . .' he added with a smile.

Impulsively her hand flew to her nose. 'Does it?' she asked, dismayed.

'Do not look so hurt and shocked. Your anger makes you more alive—you have too much of a meek look, not enough character, yet character you have. Where is your personality—you seem like a shadow. As if you must stand in the background and not come forward. As if, indeed, you are afraid to speak in case you say the wrong thing. What has happened to you?'

He was not being sarcastic; indeed, his voice was encouraging, and Penny found herself telling him the whole story—of her mother's long illness, her father's sorrow and depression, her feeling that he needed her.

'I loved him so much—I love him so much,' she hastily corrected herself, 'and I didn't mind devoting myself to him. I enjoyed it. We sold the house as my father was advised not to do heavy gardening any more, which he loved and . . . we had a small flat and then . . . then . . . as I told you, he had met Fiona and asked me if I minded if he married again. I did mind, but . . . but what could I say? Fiona is a darling and she made Dad so happy, but . . .' Penny was twisting her hands together, her eyes moist, her voice full of emotion. 'But it wasn't the same. Dad loved Fiona. I know he loved me, but . . . but he once said to me that there were many sorts of love. The love you felt for your children was quite different from the love you felt for your mother or for your wife. I know he loved me, but . . . They never made me feel that I was in the way. I just sensed it.'

'And you were probably right. You have done the best thing, Penny, in taking this job. Meeting different kinds of people, learning to stand alone and not leaning on your father. You are a wise girl—far wiser for your age than I would have thought possible. I am glad you are with us,' he said as the horses seemed to slow and they were passing down an avenue of cypress trees. 'Yes,' he repeated, 'I am glad you are with us, and I trust you will never regret it.'

Startled, she stared at him. 'Why should I regret it?'

'Because of the hatred on this island. That is why. Hatred is a terrible thing—hatred for no valid reason is even worse, and that is what we have here on Vallora. Hatred that is without sense.'

CHAPTER SEVEN

Doña Justina Melado's home was most impressive, a huge square white house surrounded by flowering trees and shrubs. The hall was lofty and cool—there was the usual terrace with pillars supporting the balcony above that ran round the house. The chimneys were fascinating, Penny thought, as a plump dark-haired woman opened the door with a smile of greeting and Juan del Riego spoke to her in Spanish before turning to Penny.

'She is expecting us, so there is no difficulty.'

'Why? Did you think she wouldn't let you see the children?'

'I thought she might try to make me see how bad for the children this is. It could, a doctor I know well said, have a traumatic effect on them. You know what that means?' He looked amused as if it was unlikely.

Penny lifted her pointed little chin, her eyes defiant. 'I worked for the Red Cross, so I do know a bit. It means a terrific shock that may not have any effect at the time and then suddenly, years later, the patient is hit and either is ill or else has . . .'

'A chip on his or her shoulder for the rest of their life? Right. That's what he meant, I think.'

They had been walking down the hall as they talked. Looking round curiously, Penny thought how very different it was from the house where she worked—or, she added to herself with a wry smile, tried to work! Here the walls were newly painted white while the paintings hanging were gay with bright colours. She stopped dead at one and Juan del Riego did the same.

'What's the trouble?' he asked.

Penny stared at the white horse jumping over a tall hedge, a small boy clinging tightly to his neck but his face bright with joy.

'There's a painting of that child in the other house. By my door . . . It fascinates me. It's so beautifully done.'

'It is good, no doubt, but I prefer not to look at it,' Juan del Riego said, his voice harsh—so harsh that she turned to stare at him.

'But . . .'

He smiled, but she could see it was an effort, for his eyes were still angry. 'But me no buts—I prefer to forget it, so I must ask you not to mention it again.' He strode ahead and she had to hurry to catch up with him.

A door was opened and they were led into a long lofty room, bright with flowered covers on chairs and couches, golden curtains and a beautiful view of the slopes down to the valleys where small white houses were scattered, huddled under wind-resisting trees.

On a chair by the window sat an old lady.

She was very upright, her back as straight as a poker; her wrinkled face looked troubled and she wore a black mantilla that matched her long black dress.

She spoke in Spanish to Juan, her face suddenly bright. He went forward quickly over the dark red carpet and bent and kissed her hand and then her cheek. He turned and beckoned to Penny.

'May I introduce the young companion I have got for the children?' he said slowly, looking at the old lady. 'Miss Trecannon.'

Doña Justina smiled and held out her hand. 'Welcome. I have been told you prefer to be called Penny?'

Penny shook hands, feeling the warmth of the old fingers as they closed round hers. 'Who told you?' she asked with a smile.

'Catalina—who else? She talks so much of *Pen-nee—Pen-nee*.'

'She's a darling, the easiest of them all.'

The old lady laughed. 'I would not think any one of them is easy.' She spoke to the waiting maid who hurried away and Doña Justina smiled at Penny. 'Please to sit down. It is good to meet you.' She looked at Juan and spoke in Spanish. He answered at once as Penny sat down obediently.

She had wondered a little how Doña Justina would accept her. She was friendly, but in a reserved way, and her eyes were full of questions. It was only natural when, as Juan had said, she loved the children so much that she should be concerned.

In a few moments the door opened and the children stood there. Catalina came first, her blonde hair streaming behind her, her eyes wary as she quickly looked round the room and then ran to Juan's arms. Techa hesitated and behind her stood the nanny holding the small boy's hand. For once, Penny thought with relief, he was not screaming.

She sat silently watching the way Juan played with the children, making them laugh while Doña Justina also sat silently, her face rapt with delight as she watched—then she looked at Penny and smiled.

'They love him as they loved their father,' she said. 'It is sad, but understandable. The marriage should never have taken place, for she is not one of us.' The words were said with sadness, not malice. Now the old lady gave Penny a really serious look. 'My son has told me that he met you. He was impressed.'

'Impressed?' Penny, suddenly embarrassed, echoed.

'Your colouring is so unlike ours. He was fascinated by the red of your hair, the paleness of your cheeks, the greenness of your eyes. I thought he was exaggerating, but now I can see he only told the truth. You are very beautiful.'

'Oh!' Penny's face was bright red.

The old lady laughed. 'No need to be so modest, dear child. You have only to look in the mirror to see what I say is the truth. It must upset Magdalena very much. She was a beauty in her youth—now that she is in her late thirties, she realises that the end is near.'

'The end?'

The old lady smiled a little sadly. 'She is no longer young and every day her reflection gets a little worse, and one day she will stare at herself and weep, for this will not be the self she thought she was. I know what I am talking about,' Doña Justina said sadly, 'for it happened to me. Alas, or perhaps by good fortune, my husband did not notice the change in me, but Magdalena has no husband now, and what man will look at her as she grows older?'

'I thought she was beautiful . . .'

'She is—but it is the last stage. Her temper makes it worse. It is sad that when we grow old, we lose our beauty. You are more fortunate with your fair skin.' Doña Justina paused and gazed at her hands thoughtfully before looking up. 'My dear child, you are young and immature. I do not wish to offend or hurt you, but I would give you a warning.' She looked out of the window to where Juan was playing with the children, little Abilio riding on Juan's shoulders and loving every moment of it.

'You will not offend me, Doña Justina,' Penny said slowly, then wondered if it sounded pompous, but talking with this old lady with her way of speech influenced her.

Doña Justina smiled. 'Thank you. I know my son is handsome—he has what I believe is called "it"—or perhaps it was called that when I was young.' She smiled. 'I am so far from the modern world these days. As I said, my son is a handsome man, very attracted by girls with red hair—' she smiled again, 'and you are young, my dear, but I must warn you. If you love Alfonso it can only mean sorrow. He is not a marrying man. He likes his pleasure, but is not interested in being tied to one woman. I would not want you hurt.'

Penny tried to hide her surprise. It had never struck her for one moment that she could fall in love with Alfonso. He was older than Juan del Riego, who was in his mid-thirties.

'It is kind of you to warn me, Doña Justina,' she said, then smiled. 'But you need not worry, because he is not my type.'

'You have a type you like?'

Penny laughed. 'No, I'm afraid not.'

'Then you are in great danger, my child. You are—? Is it nineteen years old and you have not been in love?' The old lady's black mantilla swung as she shook her head in wonder. 'You must be careful. Do not believe that your first love is your best love. When you do fall in love, my child, be sure he is the right one.'

'Oh, I will,' Penny promised, and was glad

103

that Juan del Riego and the children came into the room at that moment.

It was time, he said, to go home. Catalina looked for a moment as if she was about to cry, but the sudden arrival in the room of the nanny caused her face to change and she looked at the floor, going out meekly when told to do so.

Riding in the carriage with Juan and the children and the nanny gave Penny a chance to sit back and think for they were talking Spanish. Doña Justina had been more than kind, but obviously really worried in case the young immature girl should fall in love with Alfonso. She had said he was not the marrying kind. Frankly, Penny thought, he was handsome, amusing, yet at the same time there was something about him that had frightened her.

Yet did that really matter? Hadn't she been frightened by Juan himself, as they were driven over that high bridge with the ground so far below you could hardly see it?

What was the matter with her? she wondered. As her father had said, her imagination sometimes carried her away. Why should either of those men frighten her?

Juan del Riego turned to Penny and spoke, in English this time.

'You will dine with us tonight. We have invited some of the family to meet you. I am determined that they must see you as you

104

really are and not as lies make out.'

'How am I?' Penny asked.

He glanced at her thoughtfully. 'You are very young. You have not begun to live—you are like a child.' He watched the anger grow in her eyes. 'You are nearer to the children's age than the governess was. Incidentally, she has gone. We do not need her. Nurse will put them to bed, but you are to spend all day with them except the *siesta* time. You can do as you wish—sleep or walk in the garden or swim. You will always dine with us . . .'

'Whether I want to or not?' Penny could stand it no more—the way he laid down the law and expected it to be obeyed.

He looked amused. 'You have forgotten that I engaged you to work for me, not to do what you like.'

'And if the children's mother comes to take them away?'

'She will not do any such thing.' His voice was cold as ice. 'I have made it plain that as the children's guardian, I have the right to do what I have done and intend to do. I will not tolerate interference. She has had her choice —obey me or lose the children.'

'But she's their mother. You couldn't be so cruel!'

'Cruel?' His black eyebrows met as he frowned. 'I think it is more cruel to let them stay. The three of them are scared to death of her. She should never have had children. Not,' he added hastily, 'that I blame her for it. Some of us are born with maternal and paternal feelings. Others are born without love of this kind. They do not mean to be cruel—they don't know what love is or what the children need. Pedro did and gave them the love they needed. Now they have none at all. Another thing—*you* must give them love. Already Catalina likes you. That is a big step in the right direction. You want to have children?'

'Yes . . . well, I . . .' Penny stumbled over the words. 'Actually I haven't thought much about the future,' she confessed.

Abilio began to cry. Juan picked him up off the seat and rocked him in his arms. Penny stared silently. What an extraordinary man Juan del Riego was—a real mix-up. He could be so cruel, so arrogant, so impossible and then, suddenly, he could be kind and helpful and loving to the children. Which was the real Juan?

Just as the carriage approached the house, Juan, turned to Penny.

'I did not tell Magdalena what you told me about her visit to the day nursery, simply that she said you could enjoy a holiday as she wanted the children.'

Penny had rather dreaded the next meeting with Señora Dominguez, but his words made her feel less worried. How extraordinarily thoughtful he could be—at times!

               *   *   *

It was just as Juan had promised—when Penny
joined the others in the drawing room for
drinks before dining, Señora Dominguez was
charming, asking how Doña Justina was,
saying how the children had enjoyed their little
holiday. There were several of the family for
dinner—two good-looking men, rather elderly,
but both obviously attracted by Penny's
youthful beauty and her, to them, unusual
colouring. There was also a really beautiful girl
called Julieta Melado, tall, slender, with
masses of black hair and dark eyes. She was
only a few years older than Penny and could
speak English, so they talked quite a lot.
Julieta said that although she loved Vallora,
she also hoped one day to see the world.

'You are so lucky, you English,' she told
Penny. 'You are so free. You can do anything
you like. It is not as simple for us. Our parents
and even our great-aunt says what we may and
may not do. Fortunately I am one of the
family,' she added.

After dinner, Señora Dominguez played the
piano and Penny found herself talking to the
two elderly men, whose English was slow and
sometimes difficult to understand. Julieta was
talking to Juan, her hands on his arm as she
leant sideways towards him from her chair.
She was talking fast—Spanish, of course—her
amber-coloured dress clinging to her beautiful

107

body, her dark eyes shining, her cloud of dark hair framing her beautiful face. That was how Juan saw her, Penny knew, for he was smiling, his face relaxed, his eyes full of admiration as he talked to the beautiful girl. As for Julieta ... there was no doubt about how she felt. She was obviously deeply in love with Juan del Riego. Deeply and determined!

CHAPTER EIGHT

Juan del Riego's return to Vallora made a terrific difference, but though, on the surface, everything went smoothly, Penny still had the uncomfortable, and at times frightening, feeling of hatred that had been there since her arrival. Sometimes she told herself it was her own fault—because not knowing Spanish, how could she talk or make friends with any of the staff? Maybe they blamed her for the governess's departure—maybe they just hated anything English. But the hatred was there, all the same.

She made no attempt to teach the children, she simply played with them, making songs of the names of different objects. She was surprised at the speed with which Catalina learned the language, but Techa was still apt to start screaming over nothing at all and Abilio would immediately copy her, and then Nanny would appear and take them away, bringing them back a considerable time later. It wasn't a good atmosphere, Penny knew, either for her or for the children.

So it came as a relief when Juan del Riego told her that there was to be a fair in the town and he was taking her and the children to see it.

'It is full of noise and music,' he said with a

smile. 'I think you will enjoy it.'

'I'm sure we will,' Penny said eagerly, delighted at the chance to leave the house for a while, for cold eyes full of hatred seemed to follow her wherever she went.

The children were excited, too, and Nanny sat, stiff and silent, her mouth pursed in a disapproving button, her eyes downcast, but Juan del Riego had the children laughing happily except—Penny noticed—except for Catalina who was very quiet, sitting by Penny's side.

The town—whose name Penny could never pronounce properly despite the constant corrections made by a solemn-faced Catalina —was gay with canvas kiosks arranged in rows; everywhere there were flowers and flags and small coloured lamps that would go on at night. The road was covered with golden sand and Juan found a good place for them all to sit and watch the processions. The men who were riding horses that pranced wore short jackets and scarlet cummerbunds and leather chaps. On their heads were wide-brimmed hats, but the real beauty was the girls sitting behind them pillion-wise. The girls were lovely to look at and wore full-skirted dresses with frills and in bright colours, often with polka-dotted skirts. Then came decorated carriages, drawn by magnificent horses whose harness gleamed in the sunshine and each movement of the horse caused the silver bells to ring.

'Later we will watch the dancing,' said Juan as he led the way to one of the pavilions. 'You will have a glass of Manzanilla wine and eat *tapas*.'

'*Tapas*?' Penny echoed.

Catalina touched her arm. '*Tap-as* . . .' she said slowly, and looked round. The nanny had gone and Catalina had the small boy by her side. Now Catalina shook her head slowly, smiling at Penny. '*Tapas*.'

Juan looked amused. 'I thought you were teaching Catalina to speak English—it looks as if she's teaching you Spanish,' he frowned. 'That wasn't what I employed you for,' he reminded her.

The afternoon was even more full of life. There were men dressed in black suits with wide red cummerbunds round their middles and over their faces huge masks with two horns and a white moustache which was frightening enough for Abilio to turn to his nanny and cling to her. At that moment several fireworks went off bang and Abilio screamed. Juan took him in his arms and said something in Spanish as the men pranced by, dancing, waving sticks and wands and singing.

A tall thin man came up and spoke quietly to Juan, who nodded, handed Abilio back to the nanny and spoke to Catalina in Spanish and then to Penny in English.

'I'm afraid I must go—an urgent phone call—but I'll be back. Just keep the children out of the crowds,' he said, looking round where they were standing in a half circle made by walls, amber-coloured like the rocks around them and looking down on the road below.

The crowds got worse after he had gone and the fireworks were being tossed into the road. One went off near them. Abilio screamed, Techa began to cry and Catalina spoke crossly to her. It was then that the crowd below seemed to climb the stairs that led to where they stood. Penny and the children were nearly knocked over in the crowd, so she looked round for a way to escape. She found a narrow passage going down the back and she touched the nurse's shoulder and pointed to it. The nanny nodded, so Penny led the way. When she got to the bottom of the weaving narrow passage, she turned. Behind her were men and women, laughing, shouting, clapping their hands as they followed her, but—no children! And no nanny!

Frightened, Penny tried to make her way back again, but it was like fighting against a strong current in the sea and the people looked annoyed as she tried to push past them. She was swept down to the main road with the crowd and looked round, wondering what to do, deciding she should try to return to where they had stood when Juan left them, as he would surely expect to find them there.

It was easier said than done, for now the street was full of dancers, the girls' poppy-red frills whirling against their partners' dark suits. Castanets were clicked on the girls' fingers and people watching were shouting '*Olé—Olé!*' excitedly.

'Hi!' a voice shouted that Penny recognized. It was Mike, making his way through the crowds towards her, and followed by Valentin.

'Oh, Mike, I'm in trouble,' Penny gasped as he reached her. 'I've lost the children.'

'You've lost them?' he asked, and she told him what had happened.

'But they're all right,' Mike said. 'I saw them getting into the carriage with the nurse just now.'

'They're in the carriage?' Penny almost whispered as the relief swept through her. 'Oh, thanks be! I was really worried. Señor del Riego had told me to keep them out of the crowds, so I knew I mustn't lose sight of them, but . . .'

Valentin smiled. 'How is it you say? His bark is worse than his bite. I am sure he would realize it is not your fault.'

'I doubt it. Where was the carriage? I'd better go and join them.'

'You can't,' Mike told her. 'We saw it go away. Probably he told them to go.'

'The carriage has gone?' Penny gasped in dismay, then told herself that Mike was probably right and that Juan del Riego, hearing how Abilio and perhaps Techa also were howling, because they must have been

113

frightened when the crowd swarmed round them, had sent them. He must have been angry to find she wasn't with them.

'Look, stop worrying,' Mike told her. 'The children are fine. I saw all three of them and the nanny looked pleased. She doesn't approve of so much noise—nor does the Señora Magdalena, for that matter,' he added. 'I wouldn't mind betting she told the nanny to get the kids away as soon as she could.'

'I don't think she'd . . .' Penny stopped just in time, for she had been about to say 'dare'. What a narrow escape—for Mike must not be told that Juan del Riego had threatened to take the children away if their mother did not do what he said!

'Anyhow, you can't go back, though we'll give you a lift later,' Mike said cheerfully. 'Come with us and enjoy yourself for once.'

They went to one of the pavilions where they drank wine and ate snacks—which, Penny learned, were called *tapas*, the word Catalina had tried to teach her to say correctly.

There was the sound of music, the click of castanets, laughter, voices shouting— everywhere there was life. So very different from the drab, cold, silent house.

She was laughing at something Mike had said when a shadow came over her and Juan del Riego's impatient voice broke in.

'What have you done with the children?'

Startled, Penny looked up. He was

frowning! She told him as quickly and briefly as she could while he listened in silence.

'So you sent them home,' he said finally. 'In order to enjoy yourself?' He looked scornfully at Mike and Valentin.

'I didn't! I just told you that they vanished and Mike . . .'

'Mike?' Juan del, Riego turned to him.

'I saw them get into the carriage with the nurse. She looked pleased as a cat having some cream.' He grinned. 'Nurse Nieto doesn't approve of this type of thing, nor does Señora Dominguez, you know.'

'You are suggesting that the nurse deliberately took the children with her when she got the opportunity—and . . .' Juan del Riego stopped speaking abruptly. He stood very still, as if frozen.

Startled, Penny stared up at him. He was looking across the room, his face stiff and as pale as it could ever be. He was staring at someone . . . someone whose appearance had shocked him.

It was strange to think that such a man could be affected by anyone, so Penny looked across the room, too, to see what it could be.

The first person she saw was the Señora Dominguez herself, elegantly dressed but in an old-fashioned way with a full pleated skirt of cream chiffon and a sleeveless blouse of pale pink satin, her hair curled high up under the cream mantilla. By her side was . . .

Was the most beautiful person Penny had ever seen. Tall, slim, dark hair, dark eyes—a typical Spanish girl, but infinitely more lovely than the average girl, though she was usually lovely, too. This girl was staring across the room at Juan del Riego, lifting her hand and waving it.

The Señora and her companion began to walk across the room towards them.

'I must go,' said Juan del Riego, for the first time showing dismay, Penny thought. 'Trent, can I leave Miss Trecannon with you?'

'Gladly, sir,' Mike said with a chuckle. 'I'll bring her back later. Okay?'

'Okay.' Juan del Riego was speaking as if in a trance. His voice was slow, as if it was an effort to speak. 'Take her out to dinner, and it can go on the expense account. I don't know when I'll be back.'

He walked away slowly, his movement unlike his usual quick graceful movements, towards the two walking towards him.

Mike took Penny's arm. 'We'd better get out. We don't want to get mixed up in this affair, and the less you know the better,' he said to Penny, and almost hustled her out of the pavilion into the crowded streets, Valentin close behind.

'There is a *corrida*. Coming?' Valentin asked.

Penny shivered. 'No, thank you very much. Not for me.'

116

'It isn't cruel, you know,' Valentin assured her. 'The bulls love it.'

Penny stared at him. 'You must be joking! Who'd enjoy being teased and taunted and having darts stuck in his back?'

'You go off on your own, Valentin,' Mike said quickly. 'We'll meet later.' He named some restaurant and took Penny's arm. 'Come and watch the dancing, Penny. I know how you feel about it. What shocks me is that I've been told it's the tourists that keep the bullfights going in Spain. Here it's just an old tradition that a man has to prove himself at it.'

Relieved that Mike felt as she did, Penny went with him to watch the dancers, Mike explaining the different dances.

'That's a fandango,' he said as the girls and men danced. It was very colourful, for the girls' poppy-red frills whirled against their partners' dark suits. Penny found herself soon shouting '*Olé—Olé!*' with the rest of the crowd. Later Mike took her round the stalls and they ended up at a very pleasant restaurant, built out over the sea.

Afterwards she danced with Mike and Valentin in turn and was pleasantly sleepy by the time the carriage had taken them back to the house.

Mike walked with her to the door and knocked on it. 'That was a good day,' he said. 'Made much nicer for having you. I feel like giving Nurse a tip.' He smiled.

'Do you think the nurse had been told by ...?' She paused.

'I don't think—I'm sure. *She* wouldn't have wanted the kids around when she'd planned such a dramatic scene.' The door opened and José was there. 'Goodnight,' said Mike. 'See you.'

'Goodnight, Mike, thanks for the fun,' said Penny, wishing the butler had not chosen that moment to open the door, for what had Mike meant when he said, 'she had planned such a dramatic scene'?

What had he meant, too, when he said as Juan del Riego had walked to meet the girl who had made him behave so strangely—'we don't want to get mixed up in this affair, and the less you know the better.'

Odd things to say. And why had Juan del Riego looked so surprised, so shocked ... you could hardly say delighted. He had walked to meet the girl slowly, surely it had been a reluctant walk?

If only she knew, Penny thought, as she undressed and went to bed.

*   *   *

In the morning it was just like any other morning. Juan del Riego came to see the children soon after the nurse had brought them along to the day nursery and Juan had done his usual drawings, asking Catalina if she knew the English words for what he had drawn. Sometimes Catalina drew and asked him. It was always a pleasant interlude, for even Abilio was enjoying himself, on the rocking-horse. He called it his 'oss', which, Juan said, was a good step forward.

Penny sat, as usual, in the background, drawing a scene with several things Catalina knew in it, such as a ship, the sea, the waves, a house, but she kept glancing at Juan. The tall arrogant man who had seemed so dismayed the day before now showed no signs of it, except that his mouth was like a thin line. Only once did he look at her.

'Enjoy yourself last night?' he asked.

'Yes, thank you.'

'I thought you would. By the way,' he added, 'you haven't forgotten you said you'd stay here for a year, so there can be no question of marriage.'

Penny looked puzzled. 'There is no question of marriage.'

'Isn't there? I have an idea that Trent . . .'

'Mike is a good friend, that's all. A very good friend, too,' Penny said. 'Just because we're good friends and enjoy being together it doesn't mean that we . . .'

'Love one another?' Juan asked. 'How do you know? You admitted that you did not know what love was.'

Something stung her—perhaps his amused sarcastic voice. 'Do *you* know what love is?'

she asked angrily, and was wholly unprepared for the way his face changed.

'I thought I knew,' he said as he stood up. 'Once,' he added, and left the room, saying no more, leaving Penny feeling she shouldn't have said that—obviously it had hurt him. Was it to do with the girl yesterday? Was it perhaps also to do with the time he had said he should have rebelled but hadn't, and that it had been the mistake of his life?

CHAPTER NINE

That afternoon Penny went for her usual *siesta* walk, going down the lane that led towards the group of rocks that formed a seat for her. She enoyed sitting in the sunshine while she looked down the sloping side of the mountain to the white sandy coves. She always enjoyed the walk, for part of it was an avenue of palm trees swaying in the breeze from the Mediterranean while the cicadas were chirping gaily and the little brightly coloured birds fluttering and singing, yet it was so peaceful. The quiet house made her shiver, but out in the sunshine, admiring the lovely pink and yellow roses, the sweet-scented camellias, the gorgeous purple of the bougainvilleas was like a tonic so that when she walked back to the children she felt strong again, even eager to help them learn to speak one of the hardest languages in the world.

Wearing a pale blue cotton dress, her red hair tied back with a matching ribbon, Penny sat on the warm rocks and lifted her face to the delight of the hot sun shine coming from the incredibly beautiful blue sky. She had had a letter from her father, and one from Fiona, too. The first was an anxious letter: was Penny all right, the food didn't upset her? Were the children well-behaved—how did Señor del

Riego behave? Fiona's letter was quite different. Fiona admitted that she was bored to tears. 'I daren't tell your father that because he'd be hurt, but I can't just sit at home all day doing nothing. He's on an interesting job, but it means he's away a lot, and with you away, too—! I'll have to find a hobby—perhaps painting. I just can't sit around doing nothing. We do miss you, Penny, and I hope the job isn't proving too difficult.'

Was it proving too difficult? Penny asked herself as she watched the huge waves come pounding in to hit the rocks below. Surely the beauty of it all and . . .

The children weren't easy—not even Catalina, who was sometimes eager to learn, but at others she would retreat and sit silently, her mouth tightly closed. Even little Abilio was sweet when he forgot to scream and stroked the rocking-horse, and Techa, though she was a real little madam when she wanted attention and could scream and start off Abilio, there was something very dear about her.

But there was still a hesitation in her thoughts as she thought of Fiona's words: 'I hope you don't find the job too difficult.'

It was difficult in many ways. The Señor's strange bursts of temper, his arrogant manner of giving orders was suddenly contradicted by his amazing tenderness for the children. Yet his different kinds of behaviour meant that Penny was never at ease when she was with

122

him. She was taut and prepared for a burst of temper—and also had to control her own.

'Dreaming, as usual,' Juan del Riego commented. Penny jumped; she had not heard him come up quietly behind her.

'I . . .' she began.

Juan leapt over the rocks and came to sit by her side. He gazed at her and she caught her breath. Never had she seen such questioning eyes as his.

'Is this your favourite walk?' he asked, and she felt herself relax. 'Why?' he added.

'It's so beautiful.' Penny waved her hand expressively towards the sea, such a wonderful blue—and then to the groups of little white houses and farms in the shelter of the cliffs. 'So different from home.'

'You're not homesick?'

'No, I'm not homesick,' she said quickly. She wasn't, but she was still Dad-sick, if there could be such an expression.

'Good. I wanted to see you to tell you that tonight we're having a family party to welcome Anita back. She's been away ten years and we never expected to see her again.'

'Anita?' Penny queried.

'Yes. She was in the pavilion yesterday with Magdalena. You must have noticed her. It would be hard not to,' he added.

'Oh, that girl. She's beautiful.'

'Yes. She was beautiful when I first met her. I was twenty and she was seventeen. Fifteen years ago.' He stood up suddenly. 'You'll meet more of the family tonight.'

Why had he taken the trouble to find her to tell her this? she wondered. Then she thought she knew. 'Look, would you rather I had dinner in my room?' she asked him. 'I mean, if it's a family affair . . .'

He frowned. 'Certainly not. You are my children's friend, not a servant. I want you to meet the family and them you. It's the best way to crush the scandal.'

'Scandal?' Penny echoed.

He smiled, a twisted ugly smile. 'Of course. A pretty young girl—a so-called Spanish womaniser engaged her to teach his cousin's children how to speak English! You can imagine how the family talk. They say you are my mistress.' He laughed, a curt, surprisingly hurtful laugh. 'As if that was likely! You're not that kind of girl.'

Not the kind that would attract him? Penny wondered if that was what he meant.

'I'm most certainly not,' she said quickly.

'You don't need to tell me. I want them to see it for themselves, though. So dress up smart—but not too hippy,' he added with a smile, and left her.

She sat very still as she watched him walk away—a tall man with broad shoulders and lean hips, a man with a graceful walk, a man who could hurt and also delight at times. What was there about him that made it impossible

124

not to like him? For like him she knew she did, even though he could infuriate her at times, but there was a fascination about him. Was it his looks—the strength in his face, those eyes that asked questions, his smile . . .

She glanced at her wrist watch and began to walk home slowly down the avenue of palm trees. Suddenly from behind a huge bush of yellow flowers a man came out, catching her by the arm. It was Alfonso Melado.

'Ah—the little English miss,' he said, his fingers digging into the flesh of her arm. 'It is good to see you alone.'

'I can't stop,' Penny said quickly, for he was a big man, rather frightening as she had thought before, with that strange look on his handsome face.

'You can surely spare a moment?' Alfonso laughed. 'I see you have been talking with Juan, so why not with me?'

'His conversation was . . . was to do with my job.'

'Your job?' He chuckled. 'And how is it going? Those children will never speak English. You are wasting your time—or is it, as we think, a mere cover for a more intimate relationship?'

Her spare hand flew fast and he dropped her arm with surprise as his hand went to his cheek. 'Why, you little . . .'

'How dare you say a thing like that?' Penny was so angry it was hard to speak. 'Señor del

125

Riego merely came to tell me it would be a family gathering tonight to welcome someone home . . .'

'Anita? Ah, but of course. The beautiful adorable Anita,' Alfonso said with a smile. 'She is not my kind. I like little English girls with red hair and green eyes.' He caught hold of her.

Penny had to act fast, but she did, and jerked herself free as she hit him again.

He stood back and smiled. 'So you are going to play—how do you say it?—"hard to get"? All right, if that is your line I am agreeable. I will woo you—slowly.' He was laughing as he spoke.

'I don't want you to woo me! I don't want anything to do with you,' Penny snapped, her cheeks red with fury, her eyes shining.

'Ah, it is true, then. It is Juan with whom you wish to be? You love him?'

'Juan?' Penny was startled. 'Of course I don't!'

Alfonso laughed. 'A likely story, as they say. You have met Anita? No? We do not know why she has come back, but we can guess.' He laughed again. 'She may be beautiful, but she has never known the meaning of the word diplomacy.'

'Diplomacy?' Penny echoed.

'Yes. When Anita wants something, she must have it, at once. You do not know the story?'

'No. Look, I must go . . .'

'In a moment, but first I must tell you. When Juan was twenty, he came to stay with us. My mother invited him—why, I know not, for Juan and I have never been friends. Juan had been away for ten years, also, so he had not seen Anita grow up from a bad-tempered, skinny child as I had. They fell in love, and Juan asked her to marry him. There was a scene with Anita's father when he told Juan that she was—how do you say it?—bespoken. He had arranged for her to marry a wealthy but elderly man from the mainland. Anita hated Vallora and liked the idea of going to South America with Juan, but it was not to be.' Alfonso laughed. 'As Anita's father said, he did not want his descendants to blame him for letting them be born in a family of murderers.'

'Murderers?' Penny gasped.

'Yes—the Riego family has much to be ashamed of . . . and Juan is no different from his ancestors.'

'A murderer? Juan?' Penny said slowly. She suddenly realised that she was calling the Señor by his Christian name. She could only hope Afonso had not noticed! 'I don't believe it,' she exclaimed. The anger grew inside her. 'That's a lie!'

'What's a lie?' Alfonso asked with a smile. 'Think twice before you say such a thing. Ask any of the family—they will tell you that Juan murdered my young brother.'

Penny caught her breath. It was like being slapped in the face. It couldn't be true! Then she remembered the moment of fear she had felt as they went across the bridge that had terrified her—she had thought then that Juan was capable . . . which was absolutely absurd, she told herself angrily.

'I don't believe it,' she said to Alfonso. 'He isn't like that.'

'Wishful thinking, is it not?' Alfonso looked amused. 'So ask your good friend and my great enemy, Michael Trent.'

'Your great enemy?' Penny shook her head, her red hair swinging. 'I don't understand.'

'There is much you do not understand, and will not, because you do not wish to believe such things of the man you love.'

'I don't love him!'

'No?' Alfonso looked amused. 'Is that so?' he drawled sarcastically.

Of course she didn't love Juan del Riego, Penny was thinking angrily. He was just not her type. If anyone was, she would say Mike was—easy to talk to, pleasant to be with, sympathetic, good-tempered, but . . . But? But what was there lacking in Mike? For definitely there was something lacking. He was a good friend, but that was all.

'Why did you say Mike was your greatest enemy?' she asked the tall, handsome, amused Spaniard by her side.

He shrugged. 'Because he is. Juan got him

128

here in order to get rid of me.'

'Get rid of you?'

He nodded. 'He is trying to prove—or to make it look as if proved—that I have been embezzling money from the estates.'

'And have you?' Penny asked without thinking, then wished she hadn't.

Alfonso laughed. 'And what if I had? Vallora should be mine. My grandfather was a wicked man, without sense or understanding. You have probably heard, but he disinherited my father and handed the island to Pedro's father.' Alfonso's face was dark with anger, his eyes seeming to spit fire. 'When Pedro died, it should have been mine. It will be mine, though,' he added, his voice thick with fury and determination. 'You can tell your lover that—' he added with contempt. 'The island will be mine!'

'He is not my lover,' Penny began, then as she looked at the threatening fury on Alfonso's face, she turned and ran down the lane towards the house, afraid he might chase her, for he was a powerful man. But he didn't.

*　　　*　　　*

She was playing a game with Catalina when the day nursery door opened and Juan came in, followed by the beautiful Anita.

'Penny,' Juan said in a friendly voice, 'I thought it would be nice for you to meet

Señora Anita Llobera before the crowd arrives.' He said something in Spanish and left the room.

Anita smiled. 'Well, this must be a heartbreaking job.' She looked round and the two children gazed at her, but she said nothing to them or took any notice, as she sat down and smiled at Penny. 'Whatever made you come to this ghastly island?'

'I don't think it's ghastly,' Penny said with a smile. 'It's beautiful, and . . .'

'Boring and narrow-minded as can be.'

'Then why did you come back?' Penny asked, finding Anita surprisingly easy to talk to.

Anita shrugged her shoulders. She was wearing a white trouser suit that made her olive skin even more beautiful. 'Magdalena wrote that she would like me to visit her and I was bored with being a widow. I plan to marry again, but it is only six months and the family would be horrified. I must wait a year, but the months crawl by, so slowly—' she shrugged with a smile.

'Where have you been living?'

'Where? Everywhere. My husband was a bore, but a rich man, and fortunately for me he enjoyed travelling. You name it and I have been there.' She laughed. 'My father was a clever man. At the time I was angry and hurt. It was my darling Juan I wished to marry, but as my father said, Agusto was an old man and

130

he would die while I was still young. I would then have money enough to live as I liked or to marry any man I loved. At the time I was heart-broken.' Her beautiful face was sad. 'And so was Juan—but now . . .' she laughed happily, 'I am free—or will be in six months' time.'

So that was why Anita had come to Vallora? To marry Juan. And Magdalena must have known it and wanted to hurry it up. But why? Penny wondered.

The whole time Anita was with them, she took no notice at all of the children. It puzzled Penny, but then she remembered how Juan had defended women who were not maternally inclined. Was he thinking of Anita when he had done that? It was obvious that if ever Anita had children, she would want little to do with them. The children were playing quietly for once, but certainly not speaking in English.

'Why don't you think they'll ever speak English?' Penny asked suddenly.

Anita smiled. 'Because you do not know their mother. She will not allow it.'

'But Juan says it was their father's wish, and he . . .'

'My poor Juan! He thinks he can always get his own way, but sometimes he fails. He loved me, but he did not get me. He wishes to do what Pedro planned, but he will not succeed. He is not as strong as he thinks, nor does it make sense. We do not want Pedro's children trailing after us. Let their mother and her next husband have them.'

'Her next husband?' Penny echoed.

Anita stood up. 'You have not seen? You must wake up and watch Magdalena's face when a certain gentleman enters the room,' she said with a laugh. 'I am glad we have met, for it is good to have someone to talk to who is not of the family. I will see you tonight,' she added as she left the room.

'She's beautiful . . .' Penny said slowly.

Catalina came to lean against her. 'So are you,' she said.

Penny was startled. Catalina had usually said a single word of English—this was the first statement made of her own. Penny gave her a hug. 'Good girl,' she said, and kissed the child. 'Bless you!'

That evening Penny dressed with care, in a long gown of cream silk, embroidered with green leaves. She had felt it was rather overdone, but Fiona said it suited a redhead perfectly. Penny went down to the drawing room early, not wanting to have to walk into a crowded room with everyone staring at her. Juan, Anita and Magdalena were waiting, glasses of some deep red liquid in their hands.

Anita smiled. 'What a lovely dress,' she said, waving to a chair by her side. 'A drink for our Penny, Juan darling,' she said, smiling at the tall silent man who turned obediently to the table covered with glasses and bottles.

Anita was also in a long dress, but hers was a beautiful gold colour, decorated with deeper embroidery, while Magdalena wore black. She said something in Spanish and Anita laughed and answered in English, smiling at Penny. 'That is out of date. I wore black at the funeral, but my husband would have hated me to go on wearing it. He always said it made me look fifty years older.'

They all laughed at that, it was so absurd.

The butler opened the door and gave his little bow as he announced the guests. Penny happened to be looking at Magdalena at that moment and she saw the way Magdalena's sulky face changed—became radiant with what could only be joy.

'Come in . . . come in,' she said in Spanish. Penny had learned enough of the language to understand that as Magdalena went to meet the old lady being pushed by Alfonso in a wheelchair.

It was his mother, Doña Justina Melado, wearing a black gown and giving a friendly smile as she saw Penny.

The guests began to arrive in large numbers, and Penny was introduced to so many Delados and Dominguez and quite a few Riegos that she gave up trying to remember them. Anita was greeted by everyone and the talk and laughter was loud. Doña Justina beckoned to Penny, who felt uncomfortably aware that most of the men present were

133

looking at her with interest while their wives greeted her with an icy politeness and then ignored her, so she was glad to go and sit by the old lady's side. Penny saw that Juan had noticed and looked pleased, and she remembered that he had once said Doña Justina was the matriarch of the island and that if she approved of Penny, so would the rest of the family.

'Not that she always succeeds,' Juan had added in a—for him—strange voice. Had Doña Justina been on his side when he wanted to marry Anita and her father refused to consider it so that Doña Justina failed for once?

Anita kept close to Juan's side, smiling at him, talking to him, making it very obvious that she still loved him and that their broken romance would be repaired. Juan was his usual handsome self with a charm that obviously delighted his female relations but annoyed the men, judging by their cold unfriendly looks. Did they see him as an intruder? Were they on Alfonso's side?

'Anita is very beautiful,' Penny said, gazing across the room to where Anita stood close to Juan, laughing at something he said.

'Beauty is not everything, dear child,' the old lady said with a smile. 'Juan is old enough now to have enough sense to know that.'

'Why didn't he marry her when he first loved her?'

134

The old lady's wrinkled face looked startled and, for a moment, upset before she said with a smile: 'Her father loved her dearly. He was concerned for her future. As I think I told you, he was a widower and knew that he had not long to live. He wanted her to be looked after, and the man she married was a good man.'

'But surely, if Anita *loved* Juan . . .' Penny took a deep breath—was she asking too many questions? 'I mean—was there no other reason?'

Doña Justina's face went very pale—her hand lifted towards her heart for a moment and Penny knew that it was a question she should not have asked, so she jumped up.

'Will you excuse me for a moment, Doña Justina?' and before the old lady could speak, Penny had slipped out of the room and gone to one of the cloakrooms.

Anita was there. She smiled. 'You saw what I meant about Magdalena?'

'Magdalena?' Penny's mind was with the old lady and wishing the question had never been asked, so it took a moment or two for her to grasp what Anita meant. 'You mean . . . ?'

'Alfonso, of course. Who else? He has charm, though he leaves me cold.' Anita pretended to shiver as she tidied her elaborate hair-do. 'Juan is more my type.' She smiled. 'Which do you prefer?'

The question was unexpected and Penny answered it impulsively. 'Juan, of course.'

135

Anita chuckled. 'I agree the whole way.'

'Your English is very good,' Penny said impulsively.

'So it should be—most of the ten years we spent in countries where English was the chief language. Besides, I learned it as a child on the mainland.'

'Your father didn't mind?'

'Of course not—why should he? None of my ancestors were killed by the English.' She laughed. 'Honestly, Penny, this place gets me down at times. It's far back in the past.'

'That's what Juan said.'

'I know. There are so many things about which we agree, and that is one of them. I think he's mad to leave his cattle ranch in South America and come here just because Pedro asked him to. Why not have a good manager or hand it over to Alfonso? After all, it should be his. Why should he be punished for his father's sins? You know why his father was disinherited?' Anita began, but several elderly ladies came into the cloakroom and spoke to her in Spanish, their voices disapproving as one touched Anita's dress.

Penny slipped away and returned to Doña Justina.

She smiled at Penny. 'Come and sit down, dear. We were talking about Anita and Juan. He was young and still trained to family discipline. Today I know he would refuse to allow the girl he loved to marry simply for material reasons. He would rebel.'

It was odd, but that was the word Juan had used himself.

Alfonso, though, had said there was another reason that the marriage was impossible. He had implied that Juan's ancestors were murderers and that Juan was, too.

*   *   *

The next afternoon when the house was quiet, as everyone but Penny enjoyed the *siesta*, she decided to explore some more of the countryside. She had no desire to be pestered by Alfonso and he was too big and strong a man to risk having to fight.

It was a hot afternoon but with a delightful breeze coming from the Mediterranean, so she strolled along the earth road past the houses of the family—noticing how they were, many of them, built in forms of terraces, some being higher than the others. Then she saw what looked like an old road, half covered by weeds and odd bits of boughs. She walked down it slowly and ahead was a huge rock—strangely shaped like an egg, balancing dangerously on one end. The old road went round it and as Penny reached the other side, she caught her breath with amazement.

Never had she seen such a beautiful sight. The blue sea—the white crests of waves—a large white liner going by, several small yachts.

Far down below her was a cove and on the small plateau where she stood was a house—at least, it had been a house once. Now it was a tragic, depressing sight—with broken windows and knocked-down doors and weeds covering what must have been a beautiful garden with old tubs full of now-dead plants. It was a big house, three-storey, with the usual terrace and verandah above. What had been the front garden was not big and the ground seemed to be mostly of stone with little earth. Penny walked towards the edge and could see a terrific drop down to the cove below. The cove was not sandy, it was more a mass of rocks with the sea coming in at a terrific rate, dashing as if angry with the rocks that defied their power.

'Look out!' a deep voice called, and Penny jerked with surprise. She was not close to the edge, but Juan strode over the ground, caught hold of her by the arm and pulled her back. 'I thought you were afraid of heights,' he said accusingly.

'I wasn't near the edge.'

'You could have tripped. This is bad ground or you could have stumbled. What are you doing here?'

'I wanted to avoid Señor Alfonso Melado,' she said bluntly. 'I thought I'd take a different walk.'

'Such energy! Why choose this way?'

'It's a positive crime to miss this sunshine,

and I just looked for a path.'

'I shouldn't come here if I were you,' he told her, his voice cold.

'Why? Is there a feud or something?' she asked with a smile, for it really was absurd, some of the reasons members of the family had for not speaking to one another.

'No, just an unpleasant memory. My parents and I lived here before we left Vallora. I . . . I was about ten or eleven.'

Penny stared at him. Alfonso had told her Juan was in love with Anita when he was twenty, and it had been ten years since he left the island. And then he had said that Juan had killed a small boy—Alfonso's brother. Was that why the family had left the island?

'It's such a beautiful view and it must have been a lovely house,' Penny said. 'You must have hated going.'

His face changed, became like a mask as if he was hiding his feelings. 'I was glad to be out of this hell-hole,' he said with a startling violence.

'Why? Why did you go?' she asked, then wished she hadn't. Why must she always ask questions without thinking first?

He looked at her, a cold look as if he didn't see her. 'Because my parents went,' he said, and walked away, leaving her to stand alone, watching him go.

Penny followed him slowly. She could not believe that he had ever murdered anyone.

Despite his quick temper, she was certain he could control it.

But a boy of ten . . . Could you expect him to control his temper? She shivered and hurried away from the house. Was that why Doña Justina had looked so upset and ill when asked why Juan had not been allowed to marry Anita? If he had murdered a small boy when he was ten years old would the family ever allow him to forget it? Was that why he was hated so much?

Yet she could not believe it. She could not believe it of Juan.

CHAPTER TEN

When Juan del Riego came as usual next morning to play with the children, Penny found herself watching him. Was it true that Juan, as a boy of ten, had caused the death of Doña Justina's youngest son? If so, it could only have been by an accident—but it would explain his hatred of the house where it had happened. No wonder he hadn't wanted to talk about it. How terrible for a small boy— she could imagine how the narrow-minded family would have behaved. What a terribly cruel thing, though, to say to a boy of ten— that he was a murderer. In any case, it was obvious that Doña Justina didn't see it that way, for she was so fond of Juan, so glad to see him.

'Dreaming, as usual?' Juan asked Penny suddenly. Startled, Penny dropped the pencil with which she had been drawing a house.

'No, not exactly.'

He was frowning, his arm round Abilio. 'You feel they're learning something?'

Penny nodded, her red-gold hair swinging forward so she had to brush it back. 'Catalina especially. I think the other two are very young.'

Juan turned to the small girl, who looked at him, her eyes wide with dismay. She spoke

141

rapidly in Spanish and Juan nodded, smiling as he patted her hand. Then he turned to Penny. 'It would be advisable not to repeat what you said just now.'

Puzzled for a moment, Penny looked at him. 'You mean . . .' she paused, because the door opened and Magdalena stood there, frowning.

She spoke rapidly in Spanish, obviously angry about something. Penny stood silent, wishing she could understand. Juan was answering, his voice crisp with anger but controlled, then he turned to Penny. 'I'm afraid I must go,' and he and Magdalena left them.

Catalina came to look at Penny's house and took up the pencil and added a chimney. She looked up at Penny and said with a smile, 'Chimbley.'

Even as she spoke, Catalina turned quickly to see if the door was shut and they were alone. Was that what the child had been saying to Juan? Penny wondered. That no one must know that her English was improving! Poor little Catalina. If only her mother would see how sensible it was for the children to learn the language while young. Why did Magdalena so hate English?

Penny put her arm round Catalina. 'Our secret,' Penny said, then realised Catalina might never have heard the word. 'I will tell no one. Understand?'

Catalina nodded vigorously, her hair

142

swinging. Penny stroked it and kissed the girl's cheek.

'Good girl. Can you draw a train? I've got a picture here . . .'

*   *   *

The days slipped into weeks and life on the island was the same. Juan had remembered his plans for the children and one part of the garden was railed off for them with a climbing frame, a chute down which they could slide and land in the sand-pit, and a shallow pool in which Penny taught them to swim. Sometimes it seemed to her that Techa and Abilio had accepted her, for they rarely screamed, but it was Catalina who had the most endearing habit of sliding her hand into Penny's as they talked.

During the *siesta* time, Penny often went swimming with Mike and Valentin, sometimes in the pool but more often in the sea. There was a winding path that found its way down to the small cove of pale sand and tall palm trees that edged the beach where the sea came in, more calm here because of the huge rocks that took the first thundering of the waves. In the evenings, Penny joined the family and grew to know all the different relatives. Some were friendly to her, a few hardly spoke, and when they did, it was with disdain. Penny heard more and more about the family feuds—and stories of their ancestors of whom they were very proud indeed, and each one was certain that his or her ancestors were the finest!

Anita's words about Magdalena and Alfonso were absolutely right, Penny realised as she saw how Magdalena's face lit up and her eyes shone when he came into the room. He took little notice of her, but it was as if there was a secret liaison between them, for he would kiss her hand and she would look years younger and more beautiful as she glowed.

The most amusing thing was the battle between Julieta Melado, the great-niece of Doña Justina with whom she was staying, as both her parents had been killed in a car crash, and who had a beauty of her own, and was obviously determined to win Juan's heart, despite the arrogant and obvious way that Anita took it for granted that now she was free, there was no question but that Juan would marry her!

It was so blatant the way the two girls, each one beautiful in her own way, behaved, each one determined to get Juan, that at times Penny could hardly keep from laughing, but Juan took no notice, and was charming to both girls, seeming to divide his time to keep them satisfied.

Alfonso was Penny's biggest problem, for he persisted in following her if she went for a walk during *siesta* time. Somehow or other, he was always there, following her, refusing to

144

leave her, insisting on talking to her—always about Juan and what a selfish, money-grabbing, callous man he. was. Although there were times when she thought Juan del Riego was callous yet she knew he was not selfish—just look at the way he was concerned about the children—but Alfonso's constant and often frightening insistence on following her made her go swimming with Mike more often.

He didn't mind. He said it was more fun swimming with a red-headed beauty. Usually Valentin was with him and they would lie on the hot sand, the graceful leaves of the palm trees waving overhead, casting shadows on their bodies.

One afternoon, Penny rolled over, leaning on her arm and looking at Mike. He smiled. 'What's the problem?'

'Juan.'

Mike pulled a face. 'I guessed it would happen. You're breaking your heart over him.'

'I am not!' She sat up, folding her legs and resting her chin on her knees as she looked at him. 'I just wondered . . .'

'Wondered what?'

'Well, what does he have to do on the island? I mean, he has a lovely home in South America—couldn't he have a manager here? After all, strictly speaking, it should be Alfonso's . . .'

'It isn't *anyone's*.' Mike sat up and lit a cigarette, offering her one which she refused.

'I told you it was a lease that has gone back for generations and I think has been overlooked. Just because Alfonso's grand-father had the lease, it doesn't automatically mean that Alfonso has a right to it. The lease should go to the best man, and Juan is that. He has used a great deal of his own money, for this place when we came was a real mess. Alfonso had been supposedly helping Pedro Dominguez, and from what I can see of the books, he helped himself—Alfonso, I mean.'

'But what has Juan to do? I mean, how do you manage an island?'

Mike ran his hand through his fair hair. 'I had no idea until I came here. He does just about everything—sees that all the peasants have jobs, arranges export sales, and he's starting a pension scheme as some of the old folks are very badly off. He's arranged a small clinic as there was nothing here, anyone ill had to go to the mainland. Then he has to . . .'

Penny listened as Mike went on, fascinated. It was indeed a big job for Juan—but would he have devoted the rest of his life to looking after Vallora simply because his cousin asked him to? Somehow it didn't seem fair—Juan had a right to his own way of living.

When she said that to Mike, he agreed. 'Juan del Riego,' Mike said slowly, 'is an unusual man. He can be mad as hell one moment and darned sympathetic the next. But there is one thing I admire about him—he

146

keeps his word. He wants to sell the lease—it needn't affect the family, as they simply pay rent to the new owner of the lease.'

Penny glanced at her watch. 'I must go.' She jumped to her feet and Mike followed suit. She was startled when he put his hands on her shoulders and looked at her.

'You really mean it when you say you're not in love with him?'

She smiled. 'Of course I mean it. After all, he's much older than I am, and besides, he's going to marry Anita.'

Mike laughed. 'Or so she says.' He moved fast, taking Penny in his arms and kissing her. She was startled; for a moment she was about to push him away, but then she didn't, for there was a warmth in his kiss that frightened her. Not that she was afraid of him, but for him—he was such a darling, but . . .

His arms tightened round her, his hands moved on the bare flesh of her back.

Poor Mike, she was thinking. His kiss meant nothing to her. It could have been her father— his mouth on hers, his arms round her.

Mike must have sensed this, for he let her go. 'So you do . . .' he began, but was interrupted by an angry shout:

'You should know better than this!' It was Juan del Riego himself, almost running down the narrow weaving pathway from the plateau above them. As he came closer, they could see how furious he was. 'There are probably a dozen eyes behind binoculars watching you both at this very moment!'

Mike stiffened and stepped back from Penny. 'What's so wrong with a kiss?' he asked defiantly.

Juan stopped by their sides, his eyes aflame with fury.

'You know damned well that kissing a girl in a swim-suit on a lonely beach is just asking for local gossip. The very thing I want to protect Penny from!

Pausing for a moment, Juan turned to look at Penny, his eyes going over her critically. 'You should know better, too. I thought I made it plain I wanted no lovemaking while you were employed by me.'

It was so unjust that Penny's temper grew with each word he used.

'We were not making love!' she almost shouted.

'Then what were you doing? You were in Mike's arms, weren't you?' Juan demanded.

Penny felt the colour rising in her cheeks, but Mike spoke first.

'We were not making love. I merely kissed her.'

'Merely!' Juan's voice was thick with scorn. 'Well, there are all kinds of kisses, but I've never heard one like that called "merely" before.' He turned away. 'You're late as usual, Penny Trecannon. I suppose the chance of being alone with Mike on the beach must be too tempting. The children will be waiting for you.'

'I'm just going,' she said, picking up her towel.

'About time, too!' he snapped angrily, and left them. He hurried up the winding path, half hidden by the bushes.

Mike shrugged. 'I'm sorry, Penny.'

She smiled ruefully. 'So am I.'

'But not for the same reasons as me,' he said. 'I love you, Penny.'

'I know.' Again her cheeks burned. 'I'm fond of you, too, Mike, but . . .'

'I know—now. I was hoping . . .'

Impulsively she turned to him and put her hand on his arm. 'I wish . . . I like you so much, but . . .'

He smiled ruefully. 'So long as Señor Alfonso isn't the man you love.'

She laughed, glad of the excuse to do so without hurting Mike. 'He'd be the last person on my list. Actually, Mike, there isn't anyone— anyone at all.'

'You loved your father too much.'

She shrugged. 'Maybe I did. I'm trying to overcome that.'

'Come along. We don't want to risk the master's temper again,' Mike said, leading the way up the path. 'You'll be able to overcome that protective love you have for your father when you fall in love.'

'I wonder if I ever will,' Penny said

thoughtfully as she hurried up towards the house and the waiting children.

*   *   *

That evening, as the family had dinner with a number of visitors, Penny wondered if any of them had seen the little scene on the beach—if the local grape-vine was scattering the news around, if Juan would be told that his governess, as the family persisted in calling her, was most unsuitable to look after the children. However, no one said anything, nor was there any more than the usual animosity. She had the uncomfortable feeling that the staff were eyeing her with their usual hatred— the hatred that still upset her, though she had tried to get used to it and ignore it. Yet how could you ignore those cold dark eyes, bursting with hatred—hatred of her because of something her ancestors *might* have done!

Penny managed to slip away early that evening, for she didn't feel like talking politely to the family; Juan was besieged by Anita and Julieta who were sitting on either side of him and Magdalena was talking to a very aged, tired-looking man. Alfonso was smiling across the room at Penny and starting to move towards her. Penny was in no mood for his type of compliments and his unpleasant remarks about Juan del Riego. Even if they were true, she hated to hear them.

150

Up in her bedroom, she wrote to her father and to Fiona. It was odd, but she found she could write more easily to Fiona, telling her of Alfonso and his irritating attempt to chat her up—and Mike who was a darling but definitely not for her. Penny tried to keep out anything that might alarm her father or Fiona, so she wrote praising the climate, the beautiful scenery, but making light of the children's slowness, but she did mention Catalina's obvious fear in case her mother should hear that Catalina's English was improving. It wasn't, Penny wrote, fair to the child. She also mentioned the feuds on the island, and how Alfonso's father had been disinherited and Alfonso could not forgive Juan for having been chosen as Pedro's successor.

'It is all so absurd,' Penny wrote. 'It isn't even *their* island—they have a lease that goes back for centuries. Incidentally, Magdalena, the children's mother, is in love with Alfonso and I think he is with her, though he never shows it.'

She also wrote that the children were beginning to accept her, but: 'Juan del Riego expects the impossible. You can't teach these young children in a couple of months, particularly when you have to meet so much opposition. He's good to the children, kind and thoughtful, but he has a furious temper and can be most callous and unjust.' She stopped writing and re-read it. Had she made

151

herself sound unhappy? That would worry them, and it was the last thing she wanted to do, so she added: 'I am really enjoying myself here—it's so beautiful and so different from the life I've known before.'

It was four days later that she had a real surprise. She was in the garden with the children and Abilio was sliding down the chute, shouting gleefully. Penny thought she heard someone call her name, so she turned quickly. Wondering who it was, she moved towards the small white gate of the fence that surrounded the children's playground.

'Penny—be careful!' a shrill frightened little voice cried.

Penny stopped dead, startled. She looked down and saw that if she hadn't stopped at once, in a moment she would have tripped over a small but dangerously pointed rock half hidden by the long grass. 'Thanks . . .' she began, and stopped as she realised whose voice it was that had warned her. She turned quickly and looked at Catalina. 'You?'

The girl's eyes were wide with fear as she looked round, but there was no one in sight.

'Catalina,' Penny said very quietly, going to sit by the girl who was balanced on the wide wooden wall of the sandpit. 'No one can hear us,' Penny said very quietly. 'You spoke English—not just one word.'

Looking nervously round again, Catalina moved closer to Penny.

'Daddy taught me, but no one must know.'

Penny nodded, 'I won't tell anyone—but why mustn't they?'

'Because Mother will die.' Tears welled up in the little girl's eyes and she clutched Penny's hand, digging her fingers deep in the flesh. 'She must never know, Daddy said, and it is worse now. She will have a scene and . . . and die,' Catalina spoke slowly as if thinking of each word before she spoke it, but obviously she was quite at ease with the English language.

'Why would it upset her?' Penny almost whispered, keeping her eyes on the other two children who, for once, seemed to be playing together without quarrelling.

'She hates the English and Daddy loved them. His mother was English, you see. But we love Mother and if she goes like Daddy, we'll have no one.' Catalina sounded desolate. 'So she must never know.'

'You'd have your Uncle Juan.'

'He's all right, but not the same. Besides, Mother says he will marry Aunt Anita, and she does not like us.'

It sounded so sad that Penny put an arm round the child.

'It isn't you she doesn't like—she just doesn't like children.'

'We are children,' Catalina said simply.

Penny hugged her. 'We won't tell anyone,' she promised, and Catalina smiled, to Penny's joy. Catalina, at least, trusted her.

As Penny played with the three children, she found herself thinking of what Catalina had said. So Anita and Juan were going to marry after all.

CHAPTER ELEVEN

The next day Penny went for her favourite walk to the rocks—the walk she usually avoided in case Alfonso would be there. That day, however, she knew she was safe from his unpleasant 'wooing', as he called it, with that frightening smile on his dark face. Only that morning had Alfonso arrived with his mother, Doña Justina Melado, before driving her to visit some relative who was ill, so Penny felt quite safe.

She loved the walk, particularly the part where the track became like a weaving pencilled line, walled in by tall bushes of white, fragrant camellias whose long flowered branches stretched across the path and had to be lifted so that she could get by and the ground was soft, covered with leaves and dead flowers. The birds were singing, the cicadas giving a background of sound, and the blue sky she could only catch glimpses of through the intertwining branches above her head was cloudless.

Suddenly she heard Juan's voice and she stopped, turning, and saw him hurrying towards her.

As he reached her, he smiled. 'You wanted to tell me something?'

'I did?' She was startled.

155

He laughed. 'Changed your mind, have you? Lost your courage? What is wrong? You sent for me, so you must have something to say. Let's make our way to the rocks and sit down and then you can tell me what is wrong.'

'All right,' she said.

She hadn't sent for him, she knew that. Indeed she had nothing to tell him . . . But she had, she suddenly realised, and she would tell him about Catalina and how she loved her mother and was afraid that if she learned to speak English, her mother would die. It wasn't fair to the children to have to live in such a state—to be always afraid they would lose their mother whom, it was obvious from the way Catalina had spoken, they loved very much.

'All right,' Penny said again, and began to walk, but Juan caught hold of her arm.

'Let me lead the way,' he said, and did so, holding back the branches to let her through.

He was looking over his shoulder at her, asking her if she had spoken to Doña Justina that morning, when suddenly he gave a shout and fell forward . . . not on the ground, for there was none. He had collapsed into a narrow hole.

It all happened so swiftly that Penny hardly knew what had happened—only that Juan was out of sight. She dropped on her knees by the hole and peered in it.

'Juan . . . Juan!' she cried. 'Are you

all right?'

Vaguely she could see his body, curled up, his legs up on his chest. He didn't answer and a strange fear swept through her. Suppose he was dead?

'Juan . . . Juan . . . Juan!' she shouted, leaning over as far as she could, putting down her hand, feeling at last his hands. They were still, they made no movement as she touched them.

She sat back on her heels. What should she do? Was she strong enough to lift him out . . . should she leave him and run back to the house for help?

'Juan!' she called again.

'What is it?' he asked, his voice blurred but still sounding annoyed.

'Are you all right?' she asked.

'As all right as it's possible to be in a hole this size,' he said irritably. 'Do something to help me.'

'I will, but . . . but what can I do?'

'How the hell do I know?'

Vaguely she could see him heaving his body about.

'The damned thing is so narrow. Look, go back to the house and tell José to send out Manuel and Soldigo—' He gave a little laugh. 'You can't talk to them, I forgot that. Look, go to Magdalena—and make it quick. It's not very comfortable here.' He heaved again and stifled what sounded to Penny like a groan. It

157

must be a bad pain, she thought, to make Juan groan.

'I'll be as fast as I can,' she promised.

She stood up and ran most of the way, despite the heat. She knew Magdalena would be resting, it was *siesta*, and José, too . . .

Back at the house, she made her way to the kitchen. The staff were gathered round the table and a strangely frightening silence filled the big room as she entered it.

José stood up, his face blank. Penny thought hard—she had learned a little Spanish from Catalina, but it wouldn't be easy.

'Señor del Riego,' she said slowly, and just couldn't think of the word *fell*, if she had ever known it, so she mimed it—pretending to fall to the ground but straightening in time. 'Manuel and Soldigo, come!' Luckily she knew that last word and opened the door, beckoning to the staff.

Two men got up, both looking puzzled, but they followed her. She hurried them to the deep narrow hole and saw the shocked look on their faces, so she left them and ran back to the house as fast as she could. She knew there were several doctors on the island and the name of one who often had to come out to see Magdalena or the children.

Quickly she told him what had happened and he said he would be out at once. As Penny replaced the receiver, Magdalena came down the stairway.

'Is one of the children ill?' she asked anxiously.

Penny turned. 'No, it's Juan.' She used his name without thinking because generally when speaking to the family, she was careful to say Señor del Riego. 'He fell down a hole.'

'A hole?' Magdalena's cheeks seemed to pale. 'Where? I didn't know we had any large holes.'

'Nor did I,' said Penny, suddenly realizing something. 'I often take that walk and there's never been a hole there before.'

Magdalena shrugged her shoulders. 'Juan has many enemies.' She turned away. 'He's all right?'

Penny stared at her. How callous that was! The coldness of her voice, the lack of interest, the casual way she had asked if he was all right. 'I took Manuel and Soldigo to help him, but he's hurt . . .'

At that moment, the front door that was ajar was pushed open and Juan stood there, one foot off the ground, the arms of the two men supporting him as he hopped his way along.

'He doesn't look very bad to me,' Magdalena said scornfully. 'Certainly not bad enough to send for the doctor.'

Juan and his supporters paused. 'Who sent for a doctor?' he asked.

Penny turned and looked at him anxiously. His face was distorted a little so she knew he

159

was in pain. 'I did,' she said.

'I wish you'd mind your own business,' he said angrily. 'If there's one person I hate, it's a doctor.'

'You've hurt your foot. I didn't know how bad you were,' Penny faltered as she looked at him.

For a moment he closed his eyes. Was he fighting the pain?

It was in that moment she learned the truth. She learned something she could not believe— and yet it was true. She loved Juan!

He opened his eyes and stared at her. 'Well, as you've sent for him, I might as well see him. Now your job is to look after the children—not me, you know.'

'Yes,' she said, and a wave of depression seemed to wrap round her. Why, oh, why had she to do something so utterly stupid as to fall in love with a man like Juan? 'I'm going to get them.'

She went upstairs and when the children were playing in the garden she sat very still, watching them as she thought.

Had that hole been dug on purpose? There had never been a hole there before. Was it there for *her*? She was usually the only one who used that walk. But then she remembered something Juan had said:

'You wanted to tell me something?' and later: 'You sent for me.'

She had not sent for him—but someone

must have!

But if the hole had been made for Juan . . . ? Usually she walked in front on the few occasions they were together, as the mass of boughs across the pathway were more or less new. Normally she would have been the one to fall down the hole.

It was a frightening thought, and sitting very still, she remembered other things. How often a stone fell down the side of the cliff when she lay on the sands. Even Mike had noticed it and saw to it that she didn't lie too near the cliff.

Was it her they were trying to kill?

If so—why? What had she done?

Surely, she told herself, she was thinking melodramatically, as her parents would have teased her. No doubt some animal had dug the hole . . . after all, she hadn't taken that walk for some time.

'Penny!' Catalina called, showing her the sand castle she had made for the younger ones.

'Very good,' Penny said, and smiled. 'Clever girl!'

'Cle-ver gel . . .' Catalina repeated slowly, and gave Penny a little secret smile.

'That's right. Clever girl,' Penny repeated with a smile, and told herself that of course it was absurd to think as she had been thinking. After all, who would want to kill her? And why?

As she dressed for dinner that night, Penny wondered how Juan would be—perhaps still annoyed with her for having sent for the doctor? Yet what else should she have done? She had been so frightened as she saw him curled up in that hole.

But she dreaded those questioning eyes of his that seemed able to read her thoughts. Whatever happened, Juan must never know the truth—that though she felt he was arrogant and often callously cruel, yet she still loved him! Of all the stupid silly idiotic things to have done!

She chose her prettiest dress—the skirt pale green, long and with frills round the hem that swung as she moved. The bodice was white and close-fitting. She frowned a little as she gazed at herself in the mirror—she had hesitated about buying it, but Fiona had merely laughed and said it was perfect.

Downstairs, Penny went into the long shabby drawing-room, prepared for Juan's anger—but he wasn't there. That was a relief, but it soon vanished when she found every member of the family there wanted Penny's account of Juan's accident. Apparently Juan had damaged his ankle, but it was not serious, though the doctor had advised a few days with his leg up.

'But how could it have happened?' Anita

162

frowned as she asked. Apparently Juan had refused to see anyone and had had a bed moved down to the study so that he had no stairs to face. Needless to say, this annoyed Anita, and her manner showed it. 'Juan falling over! I can't imagine it.'

'Well, it happened,' Penny answered, feeling a little annoyed. 'There was this hole in the pathway . . .'

'But he should have seen it!' Julieta, Doña Justina's great-niece, said. 'Why wasn't he looking where he was going?'

'He turned his head to say something to me at that moment and . . . and just tripped over something and fell in,' Penny said for about the hundredth time—at least, that was how it felt to her.

'What?'

'What?' Anita and Julieta spoke at the same time, their voices annoyed, their faces angry, as if Penny had no right to be alone with their beloved Juan and that it made it even worse that he had something to say to her.

'I don't remember,' Penny admitted, and laughed because it was the truth, but she saw that neither of them believed her.

Alfonso strode over to join the group round Penny.

'Where was this hole?' he demanded in his arrogant voice, but there was a look in his eyes that made Penny shiver.

She started to tell him, but he interrupted

163

her. 'I know that pathway. There are no holes there,' he said firmly.

'There was this one.' Penny lifted her pointed little chin and stared at him. 'If you don't believe me, you can ask Manuel and Soldigo.'

'I didn't say I didn't believe you,' Alfonso said with a smile. 'I know the pathway. Your favourite walk—yet you seldom go there nowadays,' he added with a smile.

She was tempted to tell him the truth—that she avoided that pathway because she hated his habit of following her or of suddenly appearing from behind a tall bush, and his insistence on wooing her . . . but fortunately she looked round and saw the interested faces, even though many of them were malicious and accusing, but she also saw Magdalena's unhappy face.

Was she thinking that Alfonso loved Penny? Penny was sure he didn't. That was the last thing he would feel for her. Now, staring at his swarthy handsome face and those cold cruel eyes, she shivered again. She could imagine him planning to kill her . . . but why? Why? Why?

She managed to control herself and smiled. 'I like a change,' she said simply.

At that moment Doña Justina, who was sitting on the other side of the room, lifted her hand and waved to Penny, with her usual unconsciously gracious movement, so Penny seized her chance to get away from the group and hurried to her side.

'My poor child,' the old lady said gently. 'It must have been a frightening experience for you.'

'Oh, it was,' Penny said gratefully. This was the first word of sympathy she had had. 'I had such a shock. He just disappeared.'

'It must have been a deep hole.'

'Oh, it was. Long and narrow—like . . . like a coffin,' Penny said, half-closing her eyes as she remembered that terrible moment, then she opened them again and saw the distress on Justina's face. 'But he spoke almost at once,' Penny added quickly, wishing she had not used that word coffin, for it obviously upset Doña Justina. Penny managed a smile. 'Actually, he was cross with me.'

'Did he think you had pushed him in?' Doña Justina asked, and Penny was startled.

Had Juan thought that? She had been close behind him . . . but surely he wouldn't think she . . . ?

'I . . . I don't think so. I mean, why should I . . . ?'

Doña Justina smiled. 'Of course not, my dear child, but in the shock of the moment, one can think anything. What was he cross about?

'I think he was in great pain and didn't want me to know.'

The old lady slowly nodded her head. 'That

is typical of Juan. He is a proud man and does not wish to admit any weakness. He must have been angry with himself for not seeing the hole and even more annoyed because he needed the help of a woman.' She smiled. 'He is like so many men—they are the strongest . . .' She chuckled. 'Or so they like to think. He would not wish for your help,' she added.

'I couldn't help him. I tried, so he told me to fetch help and I did, but he was mad at me because I sent for the doctor,' said Penny, unaware of the wistfulness in her voice.

'My dear child, you were wise to send for the doctor. Juan could have been badly injured—it could have been serious.' As she spoke, Doña Justina was looking across the room and there was great sadness on her face.

*   *   *

The next day when the *siesta* was on and the house so still and quiet, Penny was glad to get out into the sunshine. Mike had asked her to go swimming, but she had said she didn't feel like it.

Mike had been puzzled. 'Why didn't you come to Valentin and me to help him yesterday?

'It was the *siesta*. I didn't know where you were—besides, he told me to get Manuel and Soldigo.'

'And of course whatever he says must be

obeyed,' Mike had said sarcastically, and walked away.

Penny went quickly towards the rocks, down the narrow lane to where the hole had been. She wasn't surprised to see it had been filled in, for Juan would have instructed that to be done, in case anyone else fell into it. But it had been a strange hole. What sort of animal would dig so deep a hole—or long and narrow?—just, as she had clumsily said to Doña Justina, like a coffin.

The pathway was covered with leaves and dead flowers—just as it had been the day before. As if . . . as if it had been covered on purpose, because the last time she had walked to the rocks the pathway had been clear of debris.

It was hard to find the exact place, and she was leaning down, moving the dead flowers, when a voice said:

'Just exactly what do you think you'll find?'

Penny stood up quickly, startled, shocked, and annoyed with herself, because she should have thought of Alfonso being around.

She looked at him and shivered, hoping he didn't notice, for if he knew she was afraid, he would make use of it.

'Are you deaf, little red-head?' he grinned, stretching out his hand.

Penny moved backwards quickly and lifted her chin. 'No, I am not deaf. I was merely surprised at seeing you.'

'I'm sure you were,' he said sarcastically. 'Actually,' Alfonso continued, his smile ugly, 'I thought this was our meeting place. What are you doing here?'

She knew there was danger in the air. If it was his doing—the accident, that was—then she mustn't let him know that she suspected him of trying to kill her. She thought fast and got an idea.

'I was looking for my bracelet. I was wearing it yesterday and it must have dropped in the hole.'

'What hole?' Alfonso, Penny noticed, was moving slowly towards her. Aware of danger in the air, she moved backwards as slowly, too, wondering if she could run away fast enough— or if it would set him off to doing something to kill her, strangling her, perhaps. He was smiling triumphantly. 'Do you really think we believe there was a hole? We all know that Juan attacked you and you—like so many girls of today who have been trained in self-defence—caused him to fall. Of course his pride will not allow him to admit that he had been defeated by a red-headed girl.' Alfonso laughed, and began to move a little faster towards her.

'Of course there was a hole!' Penny's voice grew shrill with the fear she felt. 'Manuel and Soldigo saw it.'

'So they say. They are Juan's slaves and would do whatever he said. But none of us

168

believes the story. Juan—born in a family of murderers and a murderer himself—must have tried to kill you and you escaped. That is what happened. We know,' he added.

'It's not true . . . of course it isn't true!' Penny's voice was even more shrill with fear and Alfonso darted forward before she could move and caught her in his arms.

She struggled, but it was like being held by bars of iron as his hands ran over her body and his mouth crushed hers roughly. She waited for his hands to reach her throat—but she fought on, struggling, kicking, while Alfonso laughed.

CHAPTER TWELVE

Penny felt exhausted as she struggled in vain and suddenly a voice shouted:

'Penny . . . Penny . . . wait for me!'

It was Mike's voice and Alfonso must have recognised it, too, for he let go of her, dropping her on to the ground and hurrying away.

'Penny!' Mike shouted again.

She was breathless and couldn't make a sound, but suddenly Mike was there, helping her to stand up, putting his arm round her for she felt absurdly weak.

'What happened . . . who was that man . . . was it Alfonso?' Mike asked anxiously. 'Did he . . . did he . . . ?'

'I thought he was going to . . .' Penny stopped; she didn't want even Mike to know she thought Alfonso planned to murder her. Mike wouldn't believe it, because it didn't make sense. Why should Alfonso want to kill her? Suddenly she was clinging to Mike and he was patting her on the back to comfort her, as if she was a child.

'There, there,' he said soothingly. 'In future you're not to go for any walks alone. Understand that?' He pretended to be stern. 'I don't like that man, and the way he's been chatting you up is . . . well . . .'

'He thinks I'm easy,' said Penny, her voice returning. 'Juan warned me about it. He said that to the Spanish, we English girls have so much freedom that we're all easy.'

'I know you're not.'

Penny managed a laugh. 'Thanks, Mike. And thanks for following me. Why did you?'

'I saw the way you went and I wondered if the hole was still there . . . then I heard you crying out and I thought the best thing was to let whoever you were with know that someone else was around.

'He let go of me at once—pushed me on the ground.'

Mike gave her a final hug before letting her go. 'You give me your word that in future you go walking with me. Right?'

Penny smiled at him. She had no idea how very young she looked, as well as frightened and also grateful. Mike knew a moment of despair. If only she loved him!

'Right, Mike, and thanks a lot.'

'My pleasure.' He gave a little bow and smiled. 'Come on, there's time for you to show me your favourite seat in the sunshine.'

'This way,' she said gaily, taking his hand and leading the way, her hand stretched back and his forward. 'Isn't it beautiful?' she asked when they finally reached the rocks where she liked to sit. There was no sign of Alfonso.

'Very beautiful,' agreed Mike, but he was not looking at the blue sea with the white waves or the mountains above them, or the bright yellow and purple flowers. He was looking at Penny.

*   *   *

It was four days before Juan was able to walk about, and even then he had a crutch to help him. He made his way slowly out to the children's playground.

'Well,' he asked Penny gruffly, 'how's it going? Making any progress?'

Penny stared at him. He looked tired—something she had never seen him look before. A flood of tenderness swept through her and she said quickly: 'I'll get you a chair.'

He frowned. 'For crying out loud, stop fussing! There's nothing the matter with me.'

'I'm sorry,' Penny said quickly. 'How do you feel?'

He scowled. 'I told you there's nothing wrong with me.' His voice rose as if he was exasperated. 'I'm sick to death of the way you women crowd round and fuss—as if delighted you've got me at your mercy.'

'I'm not . . . I don't . . .' Penny tried not to show how hurt she was. This man she loved . . . Never before had she realised just what it would be like to be in love. Now she knew! It was not the thrilling, dazzling, gorgeous feeling she had expected. It was painful, but then she had done the most foolish of all things—fallen in love with a man like Juan del Riego!

She wanted to look after him, to get him a chair; she hated the tired look on his face, the thought that he was in pain. It made her forgive him for his attitude—though he had not even thanked her for getting help so quickly.

He was speaking to the children and suddenly turned to look at her.

'Have you heard the stories on the grapevine?' he asked, his voice harsh.

She felt the colour burning in her cheeks.

'Yes.'

'Who started them? You?'

Quick fury flooded her. How could he ask such a question? Even though she loved him hopelessly, it was unforgivable.

'Of course I didn't!' she said angrily. 'You know very well I wouldn't.'

'How do I? How much of you do I really know?' Juan asked sarcastically.

'Well, you must know that I wouldn't tell such a lie—and in any case, why should I? Manuel and Soldigo saw the hole, so it's absurd to say there wasn't one, even if you . . .'

'Attacked you?' Juan's smile was cold. 'Do you honestly think you could throw me over?'

She looked up at the tall man with his broad shoulders and lean hips, his handsome dark face and those eyes, still full of questions. She was so shocked that she spoke impulsively.

'You don't really believe I'd say that, do

you?' She sounded as shocked as she felt.

'This Women's Lib business—I thought perhaps you found it a good way of showing that girls were as strong as men.' He sounded amused now, which annoyed her still more.

'You know very well I wouldn't say a thing like that. I suppose, as usual, you're defending your cousin Alfonso?'

'Alfonso?' Juan echoed, and his face became like a mask, no feeling or emotion showing. Even his questioning eyes were hidden as he half closed the eyelids. 'Where does he come into it?' he asked coldly.

'Well, he hates you and is always trying to make the family think you're bad . . .' The words seemed to burst out of her mouth and though she felt she shouldn't be saying so much, she could not stop. 'He probably said it to make us the talk of the family. Did you hear that I—that I . . . She tumbled over the words she was saying, she felt so angry. 'That I pushed you into the hole—always, of course,' she added sarcastically, 'admitting that there was such a thing as a hole.'

Juan was frowning. 'I believe you had something of a showdown with Alfonso. Mike was telling me.'

'It was no business of Mike's,' Penny said angrily. 'But your cousin is the end. I keep telling him to leave me alone and he just won't.'

'You shouldn't encourage him.'

'Me . . . encourage him?' Penny almost shrieked the words, she was so angry.

'Why don't you spend the *siesta* time with Mike and Valentin—the mere fact that you walk off alone could seem to be an invitation.'

'An invitation! Look, do you mean to say that I can't do anything alone without it seeming like an invitation? What sort of men are you all?' she demanded furiously.

'Remember you're not in England now. You're on the Isla de Vallora and must live accordingly to its rules. So in future . . .'

'Don't worry,' said Penny, turning away, for suddenly the tears were near. How could he be so thoughtless, so cruel? 'I won't go out alone until I'm back in England. Mike has made me promise that.'

'Mike has? Good, then I needn't worry,' Juan said curtly, and turned to Catalina, who had been watching them but now looked away quickly as if trying to pretend she had not been listening. He spoke to her in Spanish and then, shortly afterwards, made his way slowly back to the house.

Penny watched him go and she felt unutterably miserable. If this was love, why did people say it was so wonderful? To her, it was nothing but a pain.

*　　　*　　　*

Nor did things improve as the days passed.

Love had always meant happiness in Penny's mind, but her love for Juan merely caused difficulties. Those questioning eyes of his—his sudden sharp questions that gave her little or no time to think up an untrue answer. The realization that governed her life was the knowledge that Juan must never know how much she loved him.

For love him she did. He had only to enter the room for a cold shiver to slide down her back. If she wasn't cautious, she was afraid that her joy at seeing him would betray her— just as Magdalena's happy face when she looked at Alfonso told the world how much she loved him. Penny's whole life had changed. Now she found herself wondering how Juan's foot was, if he suffered much pain, but though the words trembled in her mouth, she dared not ask them, since it would only annoy him.

Not that he helped her at all, for he was in a bad mood. After he discarded the crutch, he had to lean on two sticks. Obviously much to his annoyance, for it was hardly dignified to go hopping around, Penny could imagine him thinking. She saw little of him, for now he visited the children in the garden in the afternoon, avoiding the staircase when he could. According to Mike, something very important was about to happen.

'It'll shock quite a few,' Mike said with a triumphant grin. 'And quite right, too. We've got a lot of work to get done first, though.

That's why he's in such a mood. Divided loyalty, if you get me.'

'Divided loyalty?' Penny repeated, puzzled. 'What does that mean?'

'Oh, come off it, Penny,' Mike had said. 'You know what I mean. He's thinking of the kids and their future—yet the other folks are his relations. Isn't blood supposed to be thicker than water?' He grinned, then.

Juan's mood seemed to affect everyone. Anita and Julieta were not speaking to one another, but both of them were almost fighting to sit next to Juan. He was polite to them, a cold impersonal politeness that Penny knew would have made her take the hint, but that they both ignored. Her afternoon *siestas* were spent with Mike and Valentin, generally on the beach, and her skin, that usually went red with too much sunshine, had achieved a pleasant tan.

Unexpectedly a visitor arrived. Unexpected to all but Juan, apparently; for one evening when Penny joined the family before dining with them, there was a strange atmosphere in the drawing room. She hesitated in the doorway, for even in that second she could feel the cold antagonism. Standing next to Juan and talking to Magdalena was a tall, heavily built man with thick, dark hair, a small pointed beard and a moustache with curled ends. He was bowing over Magdalena's hand and then he kissed it. He was speaking Spanish and, of course, Penny could not understand what he said, but the rest of the family visitors were sitting in a stone-cold silence, their faces worried, their eyes wide with dismay.

Juan saw Penny hesitating in the doorway, so he beckoned to her.

'I want to introduce you to Señor Clemente Casado,' he said, and turned to the middle-aged man by his side. 'This is the girl who is teaching the children English,' he said. *Curtly*, Penny thought unhappily; she had ceased to be a family friend, as he had hither-to called her, and now was just a governess.

The stranger kissed her hand and smiled. 'You have been asked to do the impossible, I understand,' he said gently, his voice deep and pleasant, his smile genuine.

Some of the tenseness vanished. 'It isn't exactly easy.

He chuckled. 'I can imagine. I was telling Juan that the best way is to take the children for a long holiday in England and let them play with English children. I am trying to persuade him to visit me.'

'You live in England?'

He smiled. 'I live in England—in South America—and in Spain. I am a management consultant so I go where I am required. I have a delightful house in the Lake District.'

'Oh, that is lovely,' Penny said quickly. 'But so is this island.'

'You like it here? You do not find the life

178

too dull?' He smiled. 'Too narrow, too old-fashioned?'

'I find it very strange at times,' Penny admitted, glancing quickly at Juan, who was frowning as if impatient.

'Well, I trust that if Juan and the children do visit me, you will come as well,' Señor Casado said with a smile. 'It would make us all happy.'

Anita came across the room. 'Juan,' she said accusingly, 'you haven't introduced me to Señor Casado.'

As Juan apologised and did so, Penny quietly left them and went to sit next to Doña Justina, who was alone and looking a little worried.

'What a nice man,' she said, never quite sure how to start a conversation with Doña Justina.

The old lady smiled, but there was no happiness in it. 'He appears to be both courteous and charming, but I wonder . . .'

Señor Casado had come to stay, it seemed, for he was in one of the rooms in the long corridor where Penny slept. Always she looked at the painting of the little boy and his white horse. Was it Juan, as a child? It looked like him, and yet it didn't . . . Perhaps, she had thought once, it was a painting of the small boy who had died. Yet it couldn't be, for he had been only five when he died and this boy was much older . . . Poor Juan, Penny would think as she gazed at the happy excited face of the

179

boy gazing at his horse. No wonder he had moods and could be difficult at times. It must be a terrible thing to have haunt you—even though it was an accident, for she was certain that Juan would never be a murderer!

Señor Clemente Casado was still with them at the end of two weeks. The atmosphere in the evening gathering was still as hostile to him and the family as wary as that first evening. The extraordinary thing about him, and that surprised Penny very much, was that Señor Casado always came with Juan to see the children, and looked in on his own. By some strange magic, the children immediately liked him; even little Abilio would follow him around like a shadow.

'You don't mind me interrupting you, Miss Penny?' Señor Casado asked one day.

'Of course not,' she said quickly. 'I'm delighted, especially as you speak English to them as well as Spanish. They love you. You . . .' She hesitated. Perhaps Juan would consider her rude if she asked the Señor questions, yet something made her. 'You have children,' she said, making it a statement rather than a question, for only someone well used to children could, make friends with them so quickly, she thought.

He shrugged his big heavy shoulders. 'Alas, no. It was a question of great sorrow for my wife and myself that we had no children. She died four years ago and I am lonely—very lonely. It would be good to have a family,' he said thoughtfully.

'You'd make a very good father,' Penny said, and he smiled.

'That is kind of you, Miss Penny, very kind. I wondered if I was too old.'

'Of course not.' She smiled at him. 'It hasn't anything to do with age.'

Juan gave a strange laugh. 'It sounds as if you were setting up a marriage bureau. Marriage isn't only having children, you know. There are other things to be considered.'

Señor Casado laughed. 'You are so right. It can be heaven or it can be hell.'

The two men left her, both laughing. Penny watched them go. Love was the same. It could be heaven or it could be hell. At the moment . . .

*   *   *

Three days later, Mike came across the lawn to the quiet part of the garden where the children had their playground.

'Penny, there's a dance on tomorrow night at the Granada,' he said. 'We've invited Anita and she accepted. Seems she's annoyed with Juan about something.' Mike chuckled. 'I'm not surprised at the mood he's in. Valentin seems to like Anita. He must be mad.'

'But has Anita accepted?' Penny was really surprised. Or was this part of Anita's 'thing'—

her idea of making Juan jealous?

'No. She's waiting to know if you'll go—if you will, so will she. What's making you hesitate?'

'The family disapproval. Juan has enough to worry him at the moment without me making it worse,' Penny said, then wished she hadn't. She looked quickly at Mike in case she had betrayed the truth, but he was studying his wrist watch.

'Pen-nee . . . Pen-nee!' Catalina screamed.

Penny turned round quickly. She saw that there in the shallow swimming pool lay Abilio! Right at the bottom of the pool. And he lay still—frighteningly still.

CHAPTER THIRTEEN

Thirty minutes later the ordeal was all over. Abilio was sound asleep in his little bed, having been examined by the doctor and found perfectly all right.

'Thanks to Miss Penny,' the doctor said warmly, smiling at her.

Magdalena was lying on a couch downstairs, having been given a strong sedative as she became hysterical when told how near death her youngest child had been.

'It was all your fault,' Juan said angrily to Penny. 'You're supposed to look after the children, not talk to Mike. You surely see enough of him during the *siestas*,' he added sarcastically.

'It was my fault,' Mike said quickly. 'Only we wanted to plan for this dance and . . . It's due to Penny that the child is alive. She was wonderful.'

Penny blushed. 'Well, I knew all about the kiss of life and . . . her voice was unsteady for a moment. 'I confess I was scared to death. Poor little boy!'

'Why didn't you do anything, Mike?' Juan demanded, still frowning.

'I saw how darned efficient Penny was being, so I raced up to the house and rang the doctor.'

'Very efficient, yourself,' Juan said sarcastically. 'Then you tell the child's mother and we have screams and faints and a real mess.'

'I wouldn't have told her, but she heard what I said on the phone to the doctor.'

'You can't blame her for being upset,' Penny chimed in, annoyed at Juan's callousness. 'Of course she was upset. It's not her fault . . .'

'Whose is it, then?' Juan stood, feet apart, hands on hips, his chin pushed forward aggressively as he scowled at Penny. 'Mine? Or Pedro's, who loved her despite her behaviour? She has never shown any affection at all for the children—you can see that.'

It was the truth, Penny knew. Not that it was any excuse for Juan to be so callously cruel. How could she love such a man? And yet she did. Even now, with him in a rage, she found herself looking at him lovingly, noticing the way his hair grew, the darkness of his eyes, the way he moved his hands when he got angry but kept them still when he was controlling his temper. Why did she love him? How could she love such a man? But she did.

'You said yourself that some women are made like that,' Penny said quickly, and remembering how she had thought it might be because Anita was so obviously uninterested in children. 'It's not her fault. You wouldn't blame anyone for being born with one arm, but it's no more that person's fault than it is

184

that of a mother who has no love for her children. Not that I can understand it,' she added, 'because I think they're darlings, and they certainly love you as well as Señor Casado. They love attention . . .'

'Something they have lacked since their father died,' Juan said. 'All right, Penny. Thank you for acting so swiftly and skilfully. The doctor was full of praise for your behaviour. Where did you learn how to do it?'

'I think I told you I worked for the Red Cross and we were taught all kinds of first aid.'

'A good thing for us, but please, in future—' Juan's voice was cruelly cutting as he went on, 'pay attention to your job—and Trent, save your talks for the *siestas*!'

*　　*　　*

The next morning a message came from Señora Magdalena Dominguez, requesting Penny to go and see her at once. Penny was a little worried—was Abilio's mother going to blame her for the accident, as Juan had done? However, it had to be faced, so she asked the nanny to stay with the children.

Magdalena was stretched out on a long chair on the terrace, just outside the drawing room whose French doors were wide open to let in the slight breeze from the sea.

'Please sit down,' Magdalena said. Penny obeyed, shocked as she looked at Magdalena's face. She seemed to have aged ten or twenty years overnight, her eyes were swollen and red from tears, and her hand was shaking. That was real shock and sorrow—certainly not acting as Juan would have implied. 'How can I ever thank you enough?' Magdalena began, and so did the tears. Penny moved her chair close and took hold of Magdalena's hand, holding it tightly.

'Don't worry,' she said earnestly. 'It happens to lots of small children—even in puddles. They fall down, are shocked and unable to get up. I'm only sorry I didn't notice when he fell.'

'You can't . . . have eyes . . . at the back of your head,' said Magdalena, trying to smile. 'Was Juan very angry with you?'

Penny felt uncomfortable. 'He was—rather.'

'He is so cruel, that man. He cannot understand. It is so difficult . . .' She began to cry again. 'He is so jealous—so possessive. I must not let the children be English or he will not marry me . . .'

'Juan?' Penny gasped, startled beyond words.

Magdalena's tears stopped—perhaps from shock.

'Juan? Of course not. I mean Alfonso.'

'Alfonso?' Penny echoed. 'He is jealous?'

'Terribly—but I love him.' Magdalena looked at Penny. 'It was always Alfonso I loved, but he would not marry me. I was not of the island, but that did not worry Pedro. He

loved me. He loved me so much . . .'
Magdalena's voice was unexpectedly tender as
she seemed to roll the words round in her
mouth. 'That was love. Yet I still loved
Alfonso, so to make him love me I must hate
the English, hate Juan, hate the children, too.
Perhaps you do not understand—you may
think I am a fool, but when you love . . .'

Penny nodded slowly, her hair swinging.
'No, you're not a fool. I do see how difficult it
has been for you.' She could not have
understood a few weeks ago—but since she
had realised she loved Juan, she could feel
sorry for poor Magdalena. When you love a
man . . .

'Alfonso will marry you?' Penny asked
gently.

'But of course,' said Magdalena. Was it a
little too quickly? Penny wondered. 'It is the
only way that he can rule Vallora. This has
been his dream, his whole life.' She looked
round nervously, but they were quite alone.
'He believes that in one of the coves there is a
ship that was sunk centuries ago. On board,
there are gold and silver coins. He does not
wish them to be found by anyone but himself.
He is a good deep-sea diver,' she added
proudly. 'He should have taken over the island
when Pedro died, but Juan stopped it. Alfonso
has a quick temper, but it is bitter, also . . .'
Magdalena went on talking, telling Penny of
how furious Alfonso was if he saw her kissing

her children. 'He accused me of loving my children, whom he hated because they were Pedro's, more than I loved him. He was not going to take second place in the life of the woman he married, so I had to pretend I did not love them. You think I am wrong? That the children should come first?' she asked, her voice pathetic and pleading.

Penny hesitated before answering. As a matter of fact, she did feel the children should come first. On the other hand, since she had realised just how much she loved Juan, she wasn't sure whether or not Juan would always come first in her life. Children needed you— but then perhaps a man also needed you, in his own way. How was she to judge—in this new world of hers that had so altered her views?

'When you love someone . . .' Penny said slowly. After all, if they had been Alfonso's children, it might have been different. She had heard once that one of the difficulties of adoption was that it was sometimes hard for a man to love another man's children.

Magdalena nodded. 'You are right. When you love someone, nothing else matters. But the children?'

'They love you very much.'

Penny's words made Magdalena's face suddenly become radiant. 'They do? It is true? You do not tell me that just to comfort me?'

Shaking her head, Penny smiled. 'No, honestly. Cross my heart and hope to die,' she quoted, making the gestures children often do when trying to insist that what they have said was true. 'They love you very much. Perhaps . . . perhaps when you have married Alfonso, he won't be jealous.'

'That is what I hope.' Magdalena dried her eyes. 'How can I thank you, Penny?'

'You have—by this talk.'

Magdalena looked worried. 'You will understand if I am not friendly when he is there?'

Nodding, Penny smiled. 'Of course I shall understand.' She stood up. 'I'm afraid I must go.'

'Or you'll be in trouble again. Poor you! I would not like to work for Juan.'

'He isn't always difficult,' Penny began, and stopped. Had she given away the truth?—but Magdalena showed no sign of having noticed Penny's quick defence. 'Just at the moment, he is in a bad mood.'

'Aren't we all?' Magdalena said bitterly. 'Who can tell what will happen to the island? It is of great stress to us all, as he says.'

Penny knew that 'he' in Magdalena's mind was always Alfonso! Just as in hers, 'he' was always Juan.

Penny managed to leave Magdalena by moving slowly, backwards, step by step, towards the French windows as they talked. Finally Penny could say goodbye and go inside. As she hurried through the drawing room, she stopped—for sitting on a chair, leaning forward, his bearded chin resting on his hands and his elbows on his knees, was Clemente Casado!

He stood up and followed her into the hall, then gently touched her arm. 'I had no intention of eavesdropping,' he said very quietly. 'I was hoping to see her after you left, but I heard it all. The poor soul,' he said tenderly. He shook his head sadly. 'How can she love that man? He is so bad, a liar and callous. I cannot understand.'

Penny nodded. Neither would she have understood, a short while ago. Juan was also cruel and callous and perhaps he told lies, too. Yet she still loved him, more than anything else in the world.

She paused, her feet on the lower step of the staircase as she realised something. She had not missed her father once—not even a little bit since she had realised what Juan meant to her!

'You agree?' Clemente Casado asked gently.

'Perhaps if he marries her.'

'She has no money. At least not by Alfonso's standards.'

'But the island . . .'

The tall big Spaniard smiled. 'Of course—there is always the island. We can only wait and see.'

Penny hurried up to the day nursery. Why was Clemente Casado here? What was keeping Juan so busy and so moody? Why wouldn't Mike tell her? Why were the whole family so worried about it?

As she opened the door, the nanny, who normally totally ignored her, now gave something that looked like a little bob. 'Fank . . . oo,' she said.

Catalina giggled. 'Th . . .th . . . thank you,' she said sternly.

The nanny smiled, the first smile Penny had seen on the usually stern face. Then she spoke in rapid Spanish to Catalina who stood by her side.

'She says she is sorry she can't speak English, Penny, but thank you for saving Abilio's life.'

Penny had guessed that was what the nanny was trying to say, but it was good to hear it. Had she perhaps made the first move through the cold barrier of the staff's hatred?

After the nanny had gone, Catalina put her arms round Penny's neck and kissed her, then turned to Techa and said something in Spanish, and Techa came forward with a shy little smile and tilted back her head to that Penny could kiss her. Penny's eyes stung with tears and she hugged them both.

'You must . . . teach me to . . do that,' Catalina said with her slow but good English. 'Save lives. Abilio is so silly.'

'I will,' Penny promised.

The door opened suddenly and Juan and

Anita came in.

'Are you coming to the dance tonight, Penny?' Anita, looking every bit as beautiful and elegant as usual in pale blue trews and matching shirt, asked.

Penny was startled. She had forgotten all about the dance. Actually she didn't feel in the mood for dancing, somehow. She didn't know why, but perhaps it was because she was still recovering from the shock of the day before when little Abilio had nearly died. She knew she would never forget the shock and horror she had felt when she saw his still little body covered with water, or the way her heart had pounded as she went to work on him, praying, as she did all she had been taught to do, that the boy's life was not lost. Nor had it been, and maybe she should rejoice, but she felt . . .

'I'd rather not,' she said. 'I don't feel much like dancing.'

'Why not?' Anita looked annoyed, then turned to Juan. 'Why don't you come?'

He lifted his foot that was still bandaged tightly. 'What should I do—sit and watch?' he asked with a smile. 'What a pleasant evening!'

'If Mike and Valentin are going, why not take Julieta?' Penny suggested.

'Julieta?' Anita repeated, speaking sarcastically.

'Why not?' Juan chimed in. 'A good idea. At least there'll be the two of you.' He sounded amused.

'I suppose so. I don't know why I said I'd go in the first place.'

Juan laughed. 'Frankly, Anita, I wondered which of the two men you fancied. I think Valentin is more your type.'

'He's so young,' shrugged Anita.

'He's very nice,' Penny joined in. 'Actually, Anita, he's one of the best dancers I know.'

'He is? Oh, well, perhaps. I'll go and talk to Julieta,' Anita said, and left the room, not having even looked at the three children, leaning against Penny as she sat by the table while Juan sat on the edge of it.

'Well, they seem very fond of you,' he commented, looking at the children. 'I suppose that's due to your act of gallantry yesterday.'

'Gallantry?' It was a strange sort of word to use, Penny thought.

'Why not? It must have taken quite a lot of courage to cope with Abilio yourself.'

'I didn't think of it . . . I just knew it had to be done.'

'You are always too modest,' said Juan, and Penny didn't like the way he spoke; it sounded sarcastic.

'By the way,' he went on, 'just why won't you go dancing tonight? Do you prefer to stay here in order to be near the scintillating, handsome Alfonso?'

Penny's cheeks burned. 'Of course not!'

'Then why?'

Should she tell him the truth? That not only

did she feel still too close to what might have been a tragedy but that, deep inside her, she knew that she saw more of Juan during the long evenings with the family than she did the rest of the day and that was the most important thing in her life?

A sudden desire to tell Juan everything seized her—about Alfonso and her fear that it was his doing, that fall Juan had made, the fall that had been meant for her. But the children were there—and Catalina was staring at them and she understood a great deal. So it wouldn't be wise.

'Why do you have visitors here every night?' Penny asked. 'I mean, I know they're all family, but wouldn't it be more sensible and less expensive to visit one another?'

Juan laughed. 'Of course it would. Any fool knows that, but the fact you have to understand is that you are not in the normal world but on the island of Vallora. It is the custom that goes back several centuries. The man who has charge of the island is the patriarch. It is his job to guide, protect and judge and condemn the rest of the family. They visit us as a sign of respect, but wait for an invitation. This Magdalena enjoys doing, I know, for she has studied the many feuds and rarely makes a mistake.' He shrugged. 'I know that it sounds crazy, but the family have leaned on tradition for centuries and come to us for advice and help.'

'They accept you?' Penny asked.

'Of course. They have no choice,' he said with a cold callous smile, and stood up. 'Well, bye-bye, piccaninnies . . .' He gently pulled Catalina's blonde plait, ruffled Techa's and Abilio's hair and left them.

* * *

The next week-end, Penny and the children received an invitation from Doña Justina Melado to stay with her for a few days. Naturally they accepted, and Penny found herself looking at once for the picture of the small boy and the white horse.

No, as she had thought, it was not the same boy. This one was young—about Techa's age, that would be five years old. The one who had died? But how?

The old lady loved having the children to stay and she and Penny had little time to talk until the evening. They had had a delicious dinner and sat drinking coffee in the bright clean drawing room, with glasses of sherry by their side. They talked—how they talked!— but Penny enjoyed it, for she had grown to love Doña Justina, and to feel sorry for her because a son like Alfonso must be a big worry.

It seemed he was more than that. Sitting in the quiet room, Doña Justina seemed glad to have the chance to talk.

'I always feel so guilty about my poor son,'

195

she confessed.

Penny thought at once it must be the son who died, but she was wrong, for Doña Justina went on: 'It was all my fault, though I did not—and could not—know it at the time.' She was waving her pretty little fan back and forwards as she talked. 'You see, when Diego told his father that he wished to marry me, his father was angry and refused to allow it. Apparently he and my father had fought a duel over a girl they both loved and my father won. She was my mother—but she died when I was born. Francisco Melado said my father had killed her—and the feud began. Señor Melado would have nothing to do with the Vives family. That was mine, and he said it was out of the question. In the end, however, Diego's father agreed. I don't know how Diego persuaded him. So we were married. I thought Diego loved me, but it was my money, for my mother had been wealthy and it all was inherited by me. My husband was like my poor Alfonso. Both with one idea: money! Then when my husband's father died, in his will he left the lease to Pedro's father, Fernando Dominguez, for he had never forgiven Diego. The family were shocked, but nothing could be done. The lease was in his name, passed on from his ancestors. So you see, my dear child, that it was because I married Alfonso's father that he is not in charge of Vallora today.'

'You wish he was?'

The old lady shrugged. 'I wish him to be happy, and he is not. There are many things about Alfonso that upset me. Has he told you how my youngest son died?' she asked suddenly, and saw from the startled look on Penny's face that he had. 'You were told that Juan murdered my little boy? Ah, Alfonso told you, no doubt? I thought so.' The tears rolled down her cheeks and she patted them with an embroidered handkerchief. 'My poor Alfonso,' she said slowly, and Penny sat very still as the words came out of the elderly lady's trembling mouth. It was as if she simply had to talk to someone.

It took a long time that night for Penny to get to sleep. What she had been told had frightened her still more.

CHAPTER FOURTEEN

On her return with the children, Penny found a family conference being held. Mike told her, explaining why he and Valentin couldn't spend their afternoons with her at the moment.

'But you're not to go on your own,' said Mike, his hand closing round her wrist, 'or you'll have that Alfonso after you, and I don't trust the fellow.'

'Neither do I,' Penny said, but she knew their lack of trust was for different things. Mike thought Alfonso was chatting her up; he could have no idea that she knew Alfonso was trying to kill her.

So she spent her *siestas* in her room, writing letters or reading.

There was an odd atmosphere in the house, one of anxiety, real dismay and wariness. Carriages drew up soon after ten carrying members of the family who had been called to the conference. Lunch was served to them all, but of course, Penny was out of it, for none came into the garden near the children's playground, but she could feel, in the evening gatherings, the different atmosphere. It was almost as if each person was afraid to speak in case someone heard.

Then the unbelievable happened. She was sprawled on her bed one afternoon, reading, when a knock came on her bedroom door and Maria was there with a note in her hand.

It was in Juan's sprawling arrogant writing: 'Come down immediately. Urgent,' Penny read.

Hurriedly she brushed her hair, tied it back with a pale green ribbon to match her dress, then hurried along the corridor, knowing now where the steps were, and down the staircase. She wondered where to go as she reached the hall with its enormous glass dome, but even as she hesitated, Juan came out of his study.

'Visitors—for you,' he said curtly, and led her to the drawing room.

As the door opened and she saw her visitors, Penny stopped dead, unable to believe her eyes. It couldn't be true! But it was . . .

'Daddy!' she cried, and ran forward into the tall, broad-shouldered man's arms. 'I can't believe it! Daddy . . .' she said again, then smiled at Fiona. 'I had no idea.'

'We sent a cable to Juan,' Fiona told her, 'and he sent one back saying it was quite convenient and we were most welcome.'

Penny slipped out of her father's arms and turned to Juan.

'Why didn't you tell me?'

He smiled. 'I thought you'd enjoy the surprise more. Look, I've arranged for Nanny to have the children this afternoon, so don't worry about them. A room is prepared and the luggage has been taken up already. He smiled at Fiona. 'I look forward to this evening when we meet again,' he said with a little bow, and left them.

'But this is absolutely super,' Penny smiled. 'I can't believe it! Come and see the garden and how beautiful it all is . . .'

She had no chance to speak alone to Fiona until both were dressing for dinner that night and Fiona had come in, asking help with a difficult zipper. 'Your father's no good at it,' Fiona said with a laugh.

'It's lovely to see you both—but what made you come?' Penny asked.

'Well—' Fiona looked uneasy, 'your father has been working hard, for one thing, and . . .'

'For another thing?' Penny asked with a laugh.

Fiona hesitated. 'Frankly, Penny, we were worried about you.'

'Worried—about me?'

'Yes. There was something in your letters. As if something was worrying you, but you couldn't write about it.'

For a moment Penny hesitated and then she told Fiona about her near escape from a fall in which Juan was injured. 'Normally I walk in front and the fall was meant for me and then Juan would be accused of having killed me . . .' Penny stopped, since she saw by Fiona's face that she found the whole story impossible to believe. 'I know it sounds absurd, Fiona, but . . .'

'But you're really afraid! Look, Penny love, your father is always telling us about your vivid imagination. Don't you think this strange atmosphere and the odd way the family behave has made you lose all sense . . .'

'Of proportion,' Penny finished the sentence for her. 'I know. Dad was always saying that to me.'

'This Alfonso?'

'I expect you'll meet him tonight. He used to make passes at me, but not, I'm sure, because he liked me. He just wanted to make trouble for me with Juan.'

'Juan? Is he jealous?' Fiona sounded surprised.

'Goodness, no. He's not jealous! It's just that he says I mustn't get mixed up in any scandal . . .'

'You?' Fiona began to laugh. When she stopped, she gave Penny a hug. 'Well, we're here now, so everything will be all right.'

*   *   *

So it seemed that evening as Penny's father and Fiona were introduced to the family. At once the ladies took to the good-looking Englishman while the Spanish men hovered round Fiona, speaking English to her.

The family conference went on—sometimes Penny heard angry shouts and often in the evenings, she saw that the wives had been

201

weeping. She wondered what it was all about. She had taken her father and Fiona to meet Doña Justina; they had also played with the children in the garden and were taken round the island in the carriage by Penny.

'Yes, it is beautiful,' Fiona agreed, but there was an odd note in her voice that surprised Penny. 'But?' she asked.

Fiona smiled. 'Maybe because they're living in a world of centuries ago.'

It was early one morning that Fiona walked into Penny's bedroom and woke her. 'Penny,' she said urgently, 'I must tell you something. I heard it late last night—quite by chance, and you'd gone to bed long before we did, so I didn't want to wake you . . .' Fiona's face was white and drawn and Penny sat up.

'Juan?' she demanded at once.

Fiona sat down on the edge of the bed and brushed back her hair as if weary. 'Yes and no. Last night I forgot the fan Doña Justina gave me, and when we came up to bed I went back to get it. I knew I'd left it in the library. I'd been in there earlier looking up something for your father, because he's writing an article about the island, you know. Well, I went into the library. The fan was on the floor by the window and I stooped to pick it up. The window was open and I recognized Alfonso's voice. I heard him say something that . . . that means what you told me isn't just imagination.'

'He was speaking English?'

'No, Spanish. I know!' Fiona smiled. 'No one knows I can speak Spanish—actually I can understand more than I can speak. Remember I wrote and told you how bored I was? Well, I went to a specially fast course in Spanish. I thought it would make it more fun when we came out to visit you. I never thought . . .'

'What did you hear?'

Fiona fidgeted a little. 'Well, apparently the other man was worried about the future—something to do with the possibility of the island being lost—and I heard Alfonso say he was not to worry, that everything was going to be all right. I distinctly heard him also say that the English girl must go and Juan be proved a murderer—that then Vallora would be his and all would be well.'

'So I was right. He does plan . . .' Penny slid out of bed and hastily dressed, talking as she did so. 'What did you do?'

'Well, I waited until I heard them walk away and then I hurried out. I don't think anyone saw me. Why all the rush?'

'I must go and tell Juan.'

Fiona smiled. 'Is it always Juan?'

Penny felt herself blushing. 'Is it so obvious?'

'To me, yes. To others, no. I'm not sure it's a good thing, Penny.'

Penny gave a little laugh. 'I know it's not. He just isn't the marrying kind. There are those two lovely girls you met, and even they

203

can't get him.' Penny was ready. 'I must go and find him.'

'He won't believe you.'

'He's got to,' said Penny, and managed a smile before hurrying out of the room. She had a strong feeling of fear—of something hanging over their heads. But how could Alfonso arrange it so that Juan would be accused of murdering her? Alfonso was no fool—no doubt he had it all planned.

She couldn't find Juan anywhere. Not in his study, in the dining room, not even in Mike's office. José found her looking worriedly in the rooms on the ground floor and asked her what was wrong. Fortunately Catalina had taught Penny a few words of Spanish, so she managed to say she wanted to see Señor del Riego at once and José understood. He opened the study door and ushered her into a chair, then said he would find him for her.

She waited and waited—and waited! Finally she went outside into the garden. Perhaps he went for a long walk in the short coolness of the morning. She began to walk down the garden, then stopped dead. Had she walked into a trap? Had Alfonso known that Fiona heard what he said? Had he seen her go into the library, even? Had he told José to look out for Penny Trecannon?

It was then she saw Juan, coming out of Mike's office and walking to the house. Penny began to run, but he had gone inside before

204

she reached it. Breathless and wet with the growing heat, she almost stumbled inside and went to the study. Not even knocking on the door, she opened it and went inside, closed the door and leaned against it.

Juan was stooping over the desk, sorting out some letters.

'Juan . . . Juan . . .' Penny exclaimed breathlessly. She was completely unaware that this was only the second time she had actually addressed him by his Christian name. The other time had been when he fell into the hole!

He looked up. 'There you are. José told me you were . . .'

'I had to see you, and quickly. Juan, you've got to believe me, though I know you won't . . .' She paused for a moment, then went on: 'Look, please, Juan . . . please believe me . . . I have proof . . . Fiona heard him . . .' she stammered, stumbling over the words in the endearing way she had when she was frightened as she was now. 'Look!' She grabbed his white jacket. 'Look, you must listen. Please!' She sounded desperate.

He took hold of her arms gently and looked down at her. 'What's all the panic about?' he asked. His gentleness was so surprising that for a moment she couldn't speak. Then the words tumbled out.

'Juan, he's going to kill me and then get you blamed for it.'

He looked sceptical as she had expected. 'That's a likely story. Who's he? Could it be Alfonso?'

'Yes . . . he said he was going to kill the English girl and that you would be blamed for the murder and . . .'

'Look,' Juan shook her gently, 'calm down. That is a lot of nonsense.'

'I knew you'd say that, but it isn't. Fiona heard him saying it . . . to one of the family who was worried about the future of the island . . .'

'I suppose Alfonso told you I killed his brother?' She felt the blood flood her face, making, she knew, her nose as well as her cheeks bright red.

'You believed it, of course. He has a way of making girls trust him.'

'I did not believe him!' Penny jerked herself free and folded her arms round her body tightly—a childhood habit she had always used when a difficult task was ahead. 'Juan, I didn't believe for one moment that you were a murderer.

'How kind of you,' he said sarcastically. 'I was not a murderer, but I killed his brother?'

'I . . . I thought you might have done so, but I knew it was by accident if you had. You were only ten years old at the time.'

'You are so kind,' he said with even more sarcasm. She blushed.

'I knew you wouldn't hurt anyone . . .' she

began, and stopped. He did hurt people—
though not physically. Look how he had hurt
Magdalena!

'Would you like to know the truth?' Juan
asked, and when Penny began to speak, he
lifted his hand to stop her. 'Hear my story first.
Maybe you won't believe it. You saw the house
we lived in . . . you saw the uneven rough-
stoned plateau the house was on—you saw the
terrible drop down on to the rocks?'

She nodded.

'Well, I had always wanted a white horse. It
was my tenth birthday and the horse was a
present. The stables were behind the house
and no horse was allowed in the front because
of the bad ground and the terrible drop.' He
stood very still, his eyes half closed as he
spoke. 'I can remember that horse. It was so
beautiful. Alfonso came to see it, too, and
brought his little brother with him. Alfonso
wanted to ride my horse . . .' Juan paused for a
moment. 'In a way, it was my fault. I said no—
it was my horse and I was going to have the
first ride. Also I said my father had told me
not to ride the horse until he was there . . .' He
paused, and Penny spoke.

'And Alfonso was jealous and shouted that
you wouldn't have the first ride after all, then
he dumped the little boy on the horse's back
and hit the horse's rump. The horse was
frightened and galloped round to the front.
You ran after it screaming for help, but the

horse went over the edge and both were killed,' Penny said.

Juan stared at her. 'How did you know all that?'

'Doña Justina told me.'

'She knows? But how?' Juan almost shouted.

'One of her grooms told her—only a short while ago. Why didn't you tell the truth? I mean, when you were twenty and came back.'

'Two reasons. First that when I was ten no one believed me when I said it was Alfonso. He had an alibi—cleverly done. I was called an infant murderer. I was sent to Coventry by the family. It was . . .' He shrugged his shoulders. 'I was young and more sensitive in those days.'

'And secondly? When you came back and you were twenty, wasn't it? She can't understand why you didn't tell the truth then. You knew this groom had seen it all . . .'

'I also knew that Alfonso had paid him to keep his mouth shut. I might have accused Alfonso, but his mother was very ill at the time. I didn't want to make things worse.'

'And Anita? Wasn't that one of the reasons her father wouldn't let her marry you?'

Juan laughed. 'That's Alfonso's story, not mine. Anita's father had arranged for her to make a good marriage with a wealthy, kind man, though he was old. The murder had nothing to do with it. But how did Doña Justina learn the truth?'

'It seems that when you inherited the lease from your cousin, you were very good to the staff. Many of them had not had their wages paid and you paid generously. This groom—I forget his name . . .'

'Saturnino.'

'Yes, that was it.' Penny smiled. 'Well, as I said just now, he went to Doña Justina and told her the truth. She didn't know what to do. She loves her son, but it hurts her to think of you being accused wrongly and getting a bad name. She cried as she told me. She's afraid of what he may do next. Juan, so am I. He'll destroy you if he can. He hates you so. I'm not making it up. You must believe me, Juan. He's dangerous. Really he is!' Her voice rose almost hysterically for a moment.

'Why—' Juan asked, his voice steady, 'are you so concerned for my welfare?'

'Why?' Suddenly she was crying. She turned away, hiding her eyes with her hands. 'Because . . . because . . .'

Suddenly he was close to her, holding her with one hand while with the other he gently lowered her hands so that he could see her eyes.

'Because . . .?' he said gently. 'Is it what I hope it is? Because you love me?'

'You know?' She was so startled, she could not think of hiding the truth.

'I didn't know,' he said, his voice tender. 'I could only hope.'

209

Both his arms were round her now as he held her close, kissing her cheek.

'You . . . you hoped?' Penny almost whispered.

'Right from the beginning, I hoped. You were so lovely, so sweet, and yet . . .'

'I thought you were cruel, callous and . . .'

'A murderer?' he asked in a whisper, his mouth suddenly hard against hers.

She closed her eyes. His arms tightened and suddenly her arms were round his neck, then her hand was stroking his thick dark hair.

'I love you,' Juan said. 'Will you marry me?'

'I love you,' Penny whispered in turn. 'I can't believe it, Juan. It's like a dream come true. I never thought . . . never even hoped . . . I can't believe it.'

His arms tightened round her, his mouth found hers. She wondered if it was all a dream and if she could wake up and find herself in bed and realize it hadn't happened . . .

But his body was warm and so were his lips—and he held her so tightly she could hardly breathe. Not that she minded, indeed she just wished it could go on like that for ever.

At last he let go of her, but he held her two hands tightly as he smiled at her. 'I hope your father will approve of me.'

'I know he will—he must,' Penny laughed. Never, never in all her nineteen years had she known it would be like this. 'You really love me, Juan?' she said, still finding it hard to believe it all. 'What about Anita—she seemed so sure you were going to marry her. So did Julieta.'

He laughed. 'A man likes to do the chasing. In the end, I had to tell them. Both bore me. Maybe Julieta will fancy Valentin. I've an idea he's interested. As for Anita—she flew off to England early this morning.'

'She's gone?'

'For good.' He pulled Penny close and traced her nose, her ears, her pointed little chin, and her lips with his fingers. 'Do I love you?' he said slowly. 'What do you really think?' The way he kissed her was evidence enough and she lay happily in his arms.

'Why did Anita go to England?' she asked at last.

Juan grinned. 'In search of a husband.' He chuck-led. 'There's one chasing her. He's got to start from square one as they never got on.'

'Who?'

'Alfonso.'

'Alfonso!' Penny had forgotten him. Now she stiffened in Juan's arms and, looking rather puzzled, he let her go. She looked at him. 'You're sure he went? I mean, it could be a trick. He means to kill me, Juan, and get you blamed for it. As I told you, Fiona heard him talking to one of the family . . .' She spoke desperately, for somehow he must realize the danger he was in.

Juan scooped her up in his arms again and

kissed her. 'My little rescuer,' he said tenderly. 'You can stop worrying. I saw him off in the plane myself. Last night, Clemente Casado and I talked to Alfonso. He's got a very bad record. We made it plain that he must either pay back what he embezzled or never set foot on Vallora again. He said he had no money . . .' Juan looked amused. 'He'll find it, but the island will never get it.'

'His poor mother—and Magdalena! She was so sure he would marry her.'

'Wishful thinking. I doubt if he ever intended to marry her. Besides, now she has nothing to offer him. Before it was the island.'

'Nothing?'

'The conference of the family has reached a settlement. Clemente Casado came here to judge the values of potential economics of Vallora. The firm he is consultant for wish to take over the lease. We have decided to part with it on certain conditions, such as that those who live here will not be evicted, but merely continue to pay the same rent as they do now, or a good judged price to be paid if the land their house is on is needed. It means that Pedro's wish has been carried out. The three children will have a good inheritance.'

'But poor Magdalena! She loves Alfonso so much. What will she do?'

Juan sat down, still holding Penny tightly. He leant forward and kissed her gently. 'My little do-gooder! Don't worry so much about others. Magdalena and the children are going to England. Clemente Casado is travelling with them next week. She'll stay with him and he hopes that one day she may get over her long infatuation for Alfonso, and marry him.'

'The children love him already.' Penny leant against Juan's chest. 'Everything seems to be working out. Except poor Mike.'

'Yes, poor Mike. I'm afraid we can't do anything about him, Penny, but I can get him a good job in some exciting place—we'll make a plan. The children . . .'

'The children!' Penny began, and stopped. 'I'll miss them,' she said, 'I hadn't thought of that.'

Juan laughed, pretending to bite her ear and finishing by kissing her. 'Don't worry, my darling. We'll have our own children.'

Penny laughed, her arms going round his neck, their cheeks touching.

'I hadn't thought of that. I'd like two.'

'I don't mind how many so long as they're ours,' Juan said, and kissed her again.

'Oh, Juan, however many we have, I'm sure they'll be a certain joy.'

'I'm sure,' he said, and kissed her again.

We hope you have enjoyed this Large Print book. Other Chivers Press or Thorndike Press Large Print books are available at your library or directly from the publishers.

For more information about current and forthcoming titles, please call or write, without obligation, to:

Chivers Large Print
published by BBC Audiobooks Ltd
St James House, The Square
Lower Bristol Road
Bath BA2 3BH
UK
email: bbcaudiobooks@bbc.co.uk
www.bbcaudiobooks.co.uk

OR

Thorndike Press
295 Kennedy Memorial Drive
Waterville
Maine 04901
USA
www.gale.com/thorndike
www.gale.com/wheeler

All our Large Print titles are designed for easy reading, and all our books are made to last.